NOW THAT
I SEE YOU

Emma Batchelor is a writer and author from Canberra, Australia. After completing a Bachelor of Medical Science (Hons) at the Australian National University and taking many gap years to work and travel, she eventually embraced her desire to write and created her own online publication. Emma lives part time with her partner Jesse and full time with her cat Luna. *Now That I See You* is her first novel.

NOW THAT I SEE YOU

EMMA BATCHELOR

ALLEN&UNWIN
SYDNEY · MELBOURNE · AUCKLAND · LONDON

The names of some characters have been changed. Others haven't.
Everything, however, is based in truth.

First published in 2021

Allen & Unwin
83 Alexander Street
Crows Nest NSW 2065
Australia
Phone: (61 2) 8425 0100
Email: info@allenandunwin.com
Web: www.allenandunwin.com

 A catalogue record for this book is available from the National Library of Australia

ISBN 978 1 76087 976 1

Set in 13/18pt Garamond Premier Pro by Bookhouse, Sydney
Printed and bound in Australia by SOS Print + Media

10 9 8 7 6 5 4 3

 The paper in this book is FSC® certified. FSC® promotes environmentally responsible, socially beneficial and economically viable management of the world's forests.

For the actual Jess, always

CONTENTS

US

THEM

ME

CONTENTS

US

THEM

ME

US

US

15 August, six years earlier

He was already waiting for her on the stone steps of the theatre as she attempted to walk quickly but casually towards him, tucking her long red hair behind her ears. She was late, as usual, this time because she'd spent too long choosing her outfit, putting on make-up, packing her bag for the night.

'Hi! Are you ready for our date?' She stood before him now, speaking with more confidence than she felt given that neither of them had confirmed whether this was, in fact, a date.

'Yes, I am. What's our plan?' He got to his feet, thrusting his hands into his pockets. It was still jarring for her to see him out of uniform. She liked how simple his clothes were, how they hung off his body.

'I thought we could go to the art gallery and then have dinner before we start work?'

'Sounds good.' He appreciated the way she was taking charge.

They left their bags in the theatre cloakroom and set off. It was a warm day, and they were in no particular rush as they walked through the park and around the lake, navigating cyclists and other pedestrians, discussing the books they had lent each other, their colleagues, the plan for that evening.

The exhibition was of British painters. They moved around the space together, gazing at paintings of imposing buildings, rolling hillsides and stormy seas, painfully aware of each other's proximity. She pointed out which of the paintings she had seen in their original homes, hinting at all the places she had been. He was suitably impressed, having not been anywhere much.

They re-emerged into the sunlight and wandered back the way they had come, nearly causing an accident with an oncoming cyclist by walking side by side rather than in single file. They had an early dinner at a bar where they had often gone as part of a larger work group. She noticed the unusual amount of food he ingested with each mouthful. He observed that she struggled to drink even a small cider.

'I wish we didn't have to go to work.' Besides the money, the only thing he liked about work was her, and as they had already spent the afternoon together the coming shift had even less appeal than usual.

'But if we don't go to work, we won't get to go out after work.' She wasn't very good at flirting but tried nevertheless. She was relying on the going-out portion of the evening to build up the courage to do what she had been thinking about for weeks.

'Fair point. I'm looking forward to that at least.'

She was the rostered manager that night and would be running front of house for a Shakespeare play. When allocating tasks she had decided to assign him to the bar. The power to delegate roles to particular staff members according to her whim troubled her under normal circumstances but tonight was different; she needed to preserve the physical tension from the gallery a little longer. She wanted to be able to go out to the bar and stand close to him while making a cup of tea, maybe feel her hand brush against his, and do it in plain sight of everyone else. She wondered how much the others suspected.

When the shift finally finished, the mood loosened. Staff members who hadn't been at work but were joining the festivities materialised as those who were going out got changed and those who were going home said their goodbyes. The more boisterous the atmosphere became, the more uncomfortable he felt. He snuck out for a solitary cigarette. This could be one of his last, he thought. She had said that afternoon that she would never date a smoker.

When everyone was finally ready the group made its way into town. They were careful not to walk too close to one another, their afternoon still too precious to be soiled by potential teasing from the others. He was back in the same clothes he had worn on their date while she had on yet another outfit: a figure-hugging black velvet dress, tights and boots.

At their first stop, she downed two drinks. She was a terrible drinker, and two gin and tonics in quick succession were enough to make her feel light-headed and bold. He was also drinking with purpose but, being better at it, required far more to reach a similar level of boldness.

The group, decidedly more ungainly now, moved further down the road to another club, this one with a dance floor. After one more drink and standing around for what felt like a safe amount of time, she asked him to dance. She was ordinarily a good dancer but, being quite drunk, she moved around him clumsily, her body sometimes bumping against his. He put his arms around her waist as if to steady her, before letting them settle there. She snaked her arms around his shoulders in response. They accidentally backed into a wall and dissolved into laughter, all pretence of dancing lost.

She leaned back against the wall, pulled his face towards her and kissed him.

DISCOVERY

26 July

I found some hairs last night. Long and dark. Glaring at me against the white tiles of the bathroom floor.

I had just got back from my work trip and was unpacking my toiletries and there they were.

I picked a couple up and looked at them. I rolled them between my fingers. They were dark at the roots and lighter at the ends. I felt nauseous.

I left a clump on the vanity and waited.

There was no mention of them that evening so, as we brushed and flossed before bed, I casually pointed them out.

Me: I found these hairs on the floor when I got home.

Jess: Really? I don't know anything about them.

Me: Are you sure?

Jess: Yes.

I scooped them up and put them in the bin. I didn't push it. Something told me not to. Things haven't been good between us as it is. Now that I think about it, they haven't been good since a month or so after my last overseas trip.

Jess hadn't wanted me to go. I was actually quite worried. I had even considered cancelling except that I'd been looking forward to it so much. Doing all my favourite things in all my favourite places. Getting off the Heathrow Express, walking the two blocks to the Sass, hauling my suitcase up and down the inexplicable staircases. Doing my ultimate Saturday. The walk through the mews houses into the park. Traipsing off towards Notting Hill, having breakfast at the bakery, trawling for whimsies and vintage clothes at the market before heading back past the little houses with ornate doorknockers, the flower-covered pub and the huge white townhouses until I arrived at the V&A, where I would see all the things I always saw, especially the Great Bed of Ware. Then I would go to Harrods to look at things I couldn't afford before buying tea in the food hall.

And then it was off to Paris to do all the things I liked to do there. Pain au chocolat, the flea, shopping for designer vintage, a walk around Montmartre, the cemeteries, the gardens at Versailles. I was looking forward to the time alone, interested to see how I would handle it. The two and a half weeks away would be the longest we had ever spent apart.

But Jess was worried. And that made me worried.

I still went and I had fun at first, but his messages concerned me. They were distant, uncommunicative. More so than usual, that is. There was not a single emoji to be had. I asked his mum to use her position of maternal authority to go over and check up on him. Susanne reported back that Jess seemed fine. His usual self.

But he wasn't, I knew he wasn't. I wasn't either. I couldn't write any of the articles I was supposed to be writing for a publication back home. I couldn't read any of the books I had brought with me. Even the incredible vintage YSL jacket I had unearthed at a flea market didn't excite me as much as it usually would. I missed Jess.

When I got back we agreed never to be apart for so long again. We knew it wasn't good for either of us. And after that things were lovely again. Until they weren't so lovely. And right now I don't think they are lovely at all.

29 July

I was out last night, having girly time at Xan's new house (it is quite fancy, with lots of rooms and a fireplace), and this morning I found more hairs—on the stairs this time.

I gathered them up and put them straight in the bin.

Jess was downstairs, sprawled across the couch playing a game, his fingers snapping away on the controller.

I sat on the little blue chair opposite and stared at the pictures on the wall above his head. The map of Stalingrad. The cranky whale. Sexy record babe. Sweet mushrooms. Little knights. The two girls looking out on a vast, starry sky.

Me: Is there something you want to tell me about last night?
Jess: No.

Me: Are you sure?

Jess: Yes.

He never took his eyes off the screen but that wasn't unusual. Jess has never been good at eye contact.

Something was definitely going on and as I sat there, watching his face contort with concentration, the controller still clicking, I decided I wasn't going to do what I usually do.

I am not going to smooth things over or pretend everything is okay.

I am not going to let Jess bury this.

I will be careful. I won't scare him away.

I will be subtle and keep this on the radar.

I won't let it go.

12 August

Despite my attempts at subtlety, I can tell Jess has become afraid.

There haven't been any more hairs and he is being far too nice. He came and inspected all the latest developments in the garden the first time I asked and didn't complain when I put on a trash movie in the afternoon to background the article on pre-loved fashion I was working on. When we went grocery shopping he bought the ingredients for my favourite pizza and didn't even chastise me for wandering off to look at microwave popcorn. And he bought us waffles even though they weren't on special.

I have a feeling something might happen soon, but I won't push it.

AFTERSHOCK

18 September

Jess has told me his secret.

It's big. So big I cannot even wrap my head around it.

I am in shock.

I need to sit with it before I can write any more.

I don't really know what to think.

I don't know what is going to happen.

21 September

This is what happened.

He was standing in the space between the couch, the book-shelves and the table, the silhouette of his torso visible through his t-shirt. It was one he always wore around the house, threadbare with a collection of little holes at the hip. His track pants were hanging loose around his narrow waist. They used to be mine.

He was nervous, I knew that. I had been aware of him moving about the kitchen long before he came over. Jess is usually calm and methodical, especially in the kitchen. But not this time; what I had sensed was the agitated pacing of someone trying to build up courage and that made me anxious. Also somewhat relieved.

I was curled up on my end of the couch, still in my dressing-gown—the red silk one Mumma had brought back from Vietnam, which I had somehow ripped a hole in the first time I wore it. Something was on the television; I can't recall what now. It's peculiar, the details that my jumbled brain has held fast to and those it has let go.

Jess: I feel more comfortable when I'm dressed in women's clothes.
Me: That's okay.

I was still facing the television, my heart pounding, my body tingling. I didn't look him in the eye.

Jess: Is it really?
Me: Of course.

I knew he wasn't talking about the track pants of mine he was currently wearing, or the pair of jeans I had given him years before that he had worn until they were no more than a string of threads. This was bigger than the occasional pair of pants.

I thought of the hairs I had found.

I wasn't really sure what to say, my mind felt too full and fuzzy to form proper sentences. I wasn't looking at Jess but I could sense him shuffling about. I couldn't comprehend what this really meant. For him, for me. For us.

I thought of what it must have cost him to say those words out loud, to make this admission with the knowledge that those words could be a trigger to explode our comfortable life, knowing that once said they could never be unsaid.

In those first moments, that admission felt precious to me: it was something that I alone had been deemed worthy enough to carry and I was grateful. I was grateful to finally know, but I still couldn't speak.

Jess: Do you have anything to say?

Me: Not at the moment.

Jess: Okay.

He went back to the kitchen to finish making dinner. I felt nauseous and unsure of how I would eat.

I didn't end up saying anything at all that night, which I now deeply regret.

30 September

I have felt almost robotic, going about my business on auto-pilot. I haven't been able to access my thoughts or feelings, which is strange for me. This state—while probably not brought about by shock, as it has been for me—is not uncommon for Jess. On the surface, he appears to be coping, but the release of such a long-held secret must surely be working away at him beneath his composed exterior.

Some days, Jess's declaration feels too big to deal with, so we silently agree to put it aside, to have a break and pretend everything is as it used to be. We go to work, we have dinner, we go to bed. We talk about normal things. On other days, it is all we can think about, so we attempt to unpick what a desire to dress in women's clothes means. Is it a sexual fetish, a need to transgress, or something more?

It turns out Jess has been drawn to feminine clothing since he was small, playing with his female cousins. In his teens and early twenties, he experimented with cross-dressing in private and in that context it mostly had a sexualised element. By the time we got together Jess was attempting to bury those desires, and it wasn't until years later, when I started going away more often and he found himself alone in our house, that he started to explore them again. He isn't sure where these feelings come from, or how to move forward with them; he just knows that he feels more comfortable when presenting in a feminine way and that can't be contained anymore.

On the one hand, I feel like no matter what happens it's going to be totally fine. Jess dressing a different way, looking a different way, should make no difference. I love him.

On the other hand, it could make all the difference.

What if I see him dressed as a girl and it changes everything?

What if I don't like the way he looks?

The way he acts?

What if I am not into it?

What if I don't handle it well and I make him feel bad?

What if he doesn't love me anymore because I let him down?

But I am getting ahead of myself. I feel like I have been entrusted with something fragile and there is every chance I will smash it without meaning to.

Oh god, does this mean that Jess hasn't been his true self all this time?

I can't even think about that.

7 October

We are starting to talk about gender identity. And we are reading—so, so many things. Books we have ordered, books we have borrowed, articles we have found online. Jess is poring over message boards and has been talking to people in random chat rooms. There is so much to learn. We are encountering terms neither of us have heard before so I've made myself a little glossary to help keep track of it all. I have also been telling Jess about people I grew up with at dancing and at school who express their gender differently.

I've noticed that our conversations have become more abstract and academic. We talk about theories and how they translate in broader society. What we don't talk about is how they may or may not relate to Jess specifically. Sometimes Jess wants to talk to me about what he is discovering and how he is feeling, but at other times he completely shuts me out.

I think we are both starting to realise that this is something more than a sexual fetish, that a desire to dress in feminine clothing is linked to something deeper, but we are still too afraid to acknowledge it properly. The words 'trans' and 'non-binary' have come up in a lot of our reading but Jess has been careful not to use them in relation to himself so I haven't either.

My heart aches for Jess. He must be so scared and confused.

I suggested he talk to one of his friends, someone who could offer support in a lower stakes way than I can as a partner, but Jess is adamant he doesn't want anyone else to know, which I understand. He isn't ready. It's too personal and raw. Secrets have always felt corrosive to me, like something I have to purge as quickly as possible. If I can tell at least one other person, usually Jess, then I am safe and the secret is safe. Jess, though, can keep secrets with ease. He is an expert at compartmentalising and containing.

The scope of what has been withheld still catches me off guard sometimes and I feel completely overwhelmed by it. It is sickening to realise that I might have been living with a stranger, but I take a perverse comfort in not being the only one he has lied to. Jess has spent an awful lot of time lying to himself. And to poor Susanne. I try not to imagine how she is going to feel about this when it eventually comes out.

Every so often, I find myself thinking about those hairs again.

I never thought Jess was having an affair; he hates people too much. The likelihood of him meeting someone without my knowing and then becoming intimate enough to sleep with them in our bed was too far-fetched.

Plus, having worn enough wigs back in my dancing days, I knew instantly that the hairs were synthetic.

Yet despite the only logical explanation for those hairs' appearance was that Jess had brought them in for a purpose, I never once considered that he might be cross-dressing.

Why didn't I think of that? I knew something was going on, I knew it wasn't an affair, but I never thought about Jess dressing as a woman. That seems ridiculous now.

Perhaps it was because there had never been any signs before. Besides taking a few of my hand-me-down pants, Jess had never showed an interest in anything feminine. He had a beard, he dressed in a simple but masculine way. He played video games and drank beer.

I think a part of me closed off the moment I first found those hairs. I desperately needed the secret to come out but also felt as though I wouldn't be able to cope if it did.

I was too afraid.

I was in denial.

18 October

It's been a month now since that night. I have been so up and down. It's as if I am caught in some sort of emotional hurricane and my thoughts and feelings are being hurled around within me, changing in nature with every cycle. One moment I'll feel so much love for Jess that I might burst, and then minutes later he will say something cutting and I'll deflate into a mire of self-loathing.

Last night's events represent what is becoming a classic example. Jess began painting both his fingernails and toenails and I was allowed to advise on colour combinations and assist with technique, which I enjoyed. I felt included in Jess's exploration and the process gave me the chance to touch Jess in an intimate way, something there had been decreasing opportunities for. I felt loving and mushy. It didn't take long for things to turn, however, and when I suggested a better method for nail painting Jess was hurt and became angry. He didn't speak to me for the rest of the evening, leaving me feeling sick with guilt and disgusted with myself. I had been too critical.

Overall, Jess's gestures have been growing steadily more feminine. Delicate hands, cocked hips, a shifting of weight. It's strange. Sometimes I feel uncomfortable because these mannerisms are so unexpected from him, almost the opposite of how he had carried himself previously. It wasn't as though his demeanour was hyper-masculine before, but there was definitely something distinctly male about him. I wonder now if that air of masculinity was put on and these feminine gestures are the more natural ones.

Jess has said he isn't ready to show me what he looks like femme and, if I am honest, I'm not ready either. It feels like a tipping point that we can't come back from. I think Jess might be dressing up while I am out, but I don't know for sure because we aren't really talking about it. I always text to tell him when I am coming home just in case. He is so sensitive about anything feminine that I think he feels safer keeping it to himself for now.

As difficult as this last month has been, though, I feel as if, after all these years together, I am finally being allowed a glimpse behind Jess's carefully constructed persona—one that I hadn't even been aware was a construction. If we can manage to navigate this, Jess's admission might end up bringing us closer together. Perhaps we will be able to connect in a way we haven't before. Perhaps everything will be fine.

20 November

Things are not good at all.

Jess is continuing to withdraw and I am not coping well with that withdrawal. The resulting space between us often feels too big to traverse.

I want to support him but my attempts to reach out, to research, to be a sounding board, are not working. I've suggested again that it might help to talk to one of his friends but that is still off the table.

Jess has always been somewhat distant emotionally, more so when he is stressed, but since his disclosure, his increased irritability, reduced eye contact and periods of complete shutdown are next level, at least in my experience of him. I considered messaging Susanne, just to say that Jess wasn't in a good place and I could do with some help, but I've decided to hold off for now.

I've had an idea that I think might help us both. Instead of stumbling through difficult in-person interactions, it might be easier to write down the more complex things. In our present situation, I don't seem to be as good at verbal communication as I thought I was. Everything I say seems to come out wrong.

Anyway, I think a correspondence might be the answer. I want to understand, I want to help.

I can do this. I *can* help.

TO: **Jess**

FROM: **Me**

Subject: An email

Hello my love,

I've been doing a lot of reading this week, more of the things you suggested and other things I've found. I read one of the articles you sent me twice. It didn't make me cry but I can see why it moved you. It was beautiful.

I've actually been finding it difficult to come across things from my perspective. There is so much out there for you, but not so much for me. If I do manage to find something it turns out to be incredibly depressing in one way or another and I don't find that helpful.

I read quite a few articles about very young couples who took it all in their stride and had no problems whatsoever, which made me feel bad. Like I am old, narrow and selfish. But I am glad things are easier for younger people and that sexuality and gender expression are more readily fluid for them.

I found something that was written by a person who was non-binary with a heterosexual boyfriend. They talked about the process of working out the role gender played in their relationship before ultimately realising that they weren't comfortable being in a sexual relationship anymore. They concluded that it didn't make either of them a bad person, or less open-minded, just that it wasn't the right relationship for them at that time. Oh, to be so philosophical and sensible.

I spent a lot of time on a message board where other women in similar situations to mine were airing their grievances. I didn't find much comfort in that as they had all decided to leave their partners after they came out as trans. One woman was complaining about her partner wearing her clothes without asking, which was apparently the last straw. The only thing I really related to was their discussion on grief and mourning. I do feel like I am grieving the life I thought I was living, the future I thought I would have. Maybe I just found the wrong message thread.

There was only one story I found that came close to what I am feeling. It was a woman whose husband came out as trans when their kids were in their late teens. The questions she asked herself are essentially the same ones we have been asking ourselves. Depending on what happens, can we stay together? Can I still find you attractive as a woman? If not, do we try to live together as friends? Is that even something I would want? Would we separate?

She talked about the difficulties couples in this situation find themselves facing. Nobody has done anything wrong. They still love each other, and they want to be together, but they aren't able to because they can't remain attracted to each other. She came to the conclusion that she didn't want to be with anyone else, that she couldn't imagine a life with anyone else, so, as hard as it was going to be, she would stay and figure something out.

This is what I want to do too. I want to stay. Like that woman, I can't imagine a life with anyone else. When I think of my future it is of us together. The only option I feel I have is to try.

Something else this woman talked about was what her husband's transition meant for her own sexuality and people's perception of it. She knew she was a heterosexual woman but was aware that from now on people would assume she was a lesbian.

I think I need to give this some more thought. I've never considered myself as anything other than a heterosexual woman but I'm starting to think maybe that isn't the case. Anyway, I need to do more reading and thinking about that.

I love you very much.

Yours, always.

I'm at work but I can't focus. I am pretending to write an important report on the impact of one of our grant programs but really I am just trying to sort myself out. I've had two pots of tea already and peed three times. Each time I went to the bathroom I sat there for a good five minutes: first trying not to cry, then having a little cry, then getting myself together to go back to my desk.

Last night was our sexversary. That day is usually a very good day as we celebrate with lots of lovely sex.

This year, I thought things had started off well. I had sent Jess the first email of our correspondence, which felt productive. I had worried that writing to each other might feel like a regression, but I was relieved to find it didn't. Through my writing I felt I could be all the things I couldn't be in person: gentle, considered, communicative.

When we got home we talked through our thoughts of the day, how Jess was feeling. He told me that he is starting to think that he is non-binary and has been thinking about pronouns. He spread his hands out before me and said if one little finger was male and the other was female, he felt like he was somewhere between the middle and ring finger on the female end. Jess being able to say that felt like a big moment. We didn't talk about what the implications of being non-binary might be; for the moment it was enough that he had found a description that best explained how he was feeling.

However, as seems inevitable these days, things went rapidly downhill from there. Buoyed by Jess's openness, I brought up our sexversary. Jess said he couldn't think about that right now, that he had too many other things to think about and sex wasn't one of them. I felt silly and selfish.

Since Jess's admission, we have had very little physical contact. A little incidental, no intimate and definitely nothing sexual.

Even though things are so fraught, my sexual desire hasn't disappeared.

I still find boy Jess sexy.

I still want to have sex.

But those feelings and desires seem to be forbidden and I find it confusing to be told off for something that used to be welcome and positive. Probably I am being unfair.

I think Jess wants me to act like him questioning his gender is no big deal, to behave as if it doesn't affect our relationship or have an impact on our lives. I can understand why he wants me to do that: he wants me to validate the way he feels, to alleviate his fears, to make everything okay. And I am trying to put my feelings aside to support him, but at the end of the day this *does* affect our lives. I am scared and uncertain and sometimes I want to have sex with my partner, and I want the space to feel that.

TO: Jess

FROM: Me

Subject: Another email

Hello my love,

I want so much to be all the things you asked of me last night. To step back, to give you space, to be more of a friend than your partner. To be strong for you while you figure these things out. I know I said I could do it, but if I am honest I said that because I knew that was what you needed to hear.

I don't know if I can do it, really, but I am going to try.

I feel overwhelmed and I feel guilty that I can't react to this and support you in the way you need me to.

I also feel guilty for feeling all of this given what you are experiencing yourself.

But I want you to know that I love you so much. None of this changes the way I feel about you and I will always keep trying.

25 November

Our evenings are becoming more and more unbearable. Jess continues to be withdrawn and at times aggressive. Maybe aggressive is too strong a word. Cranky. Snappy. Cutting. Those are probably more accurate.

Nothing I say seems to be the right thing. Nothing I do is the right thing. I am constantly in the wrong and always in trouble.

I have decided that I am going to see a psychologist. Jess has been encouraging me to go because my being depressed all the time is making him feel worse. I desperately need to talk to someone about what is going on. If I could just learn to cope with it all better I might then be able to help Jess properly.

I've never been to a psychologist before. I talked to my friend Clara, who had been to see one, and she explained the process to me. I didn't tell her why I needed to go, of course; I just told her that I hadn't been feeling well and thought it would be good to get some external advice. I felt guilty for being so guarded about my problems when she had been so open about hers, but I had to keep Jess's secret. Clara advised me to see my doctor first so I could be put on a mental health plan, which would mean my sessions wouldn't be so expensive. This was an excellent tip.

Speaking to Clara has made me more comfortable with the practicalities but I am still concerned about having to speak for an hour about my personal business. I'm nervous about being emotional and vulnerable in front of a stranger. I'm anxious, too, about having my actions and behaviour critiqued. I think I am also ashamed of not being able to cope and needing help.

Anyway, I'm seeing my doctor tomorrow for a mental health plan. Hopefully I'll keep it together.

26 November

The doctor's appointment went well, thank goodness.

I filled out a long questionnaire about my mood and the results weren't great but they're not dire.

I've got a referral to a psychologist near my office. I'll build up to make a booking.

6 December

I have survived my thirtieth birthday.

The day itself was quiet. I spent the morning at home resting and reading before having lunch with Mumma, Nanny and Poppy. This was followed by more resting and reading, and then dinner at a restaurant with the rest of the family—except for my brother dearest, of course. James had sent me a beautiful email that made me cry and we ended up talking for over an hour when the time difference between here and Berlin wasn't so bad.

Dinner involved Jess, Susanne, her partner Alex, and Mumma. Even Daddy put in a rare special appearance. Alex took charge of ordering because that is his area of expertise, and as we ate and drank the parents reminisced about their own thirtieth birthdays. Everyone agreed that I had achieved many things and was very advanced, which was too kind and made me feel awkward.

Susanne noticed Jess had painted his nails and I eavesdropped on their conversation.

Susanne: You've started painting your nails!
Jess: I guess. It's something I'm trying.

She reached out to hold his hand, but Jess withdrew it and put it under the table. Susanne was used to this sort of behaviour and didn't seem to mind. I half hoped that she would delve deeper, that Jess would be pushed to say something, but she didn't. Susanne knows even better than I do when not to push.

8 December

Last night the celebrations continued with a party. I had wanted to cancel, but Jess had already planned a whole menu and the invitations had gone out months ago so we had to go ahead. I had ordered two different dresses for the party, neither of which looked any good, so I wore a multicoloured see-through dress belonging to Mumma, a veil and no shoes.

Jess loves looking after people and making sure they have a good time. Playing host allows him to demonstrate he cares while maintaining distance. He made pulled pork sliders, pan-fried haloumi, cakes, cookies and numerous other snacks which we arranged aesthetically all over the table. My specific contribution was to arrange my presents prettily on the stairs.

The house was full of people, mostly my friends, but a few of Jess's too. Some were downstairs eating; others were outside in the garden smoking and drinking. Some were upstairs playing with the clothes, shoes and bags in my dressing room, trying pieces on and taking photos. I flitted between them all while Jess stayed mainly in the kitchen or in the garden with his friends.

Although I was touched that so many people had come to celebrate with me, I felt as though I was pretending to be happy most of the time, that in concealing all of the life-altering stuff going on I was being false with everyone. I felt best tucked away upstairs in my dressing room surrounded by all my beautiful things with only a handful of people. It is not in my nature to withhold or to conceal and I find it difficult and painful to do so with people I care about.

Throughout the evening Jess became much more comfortable and feminine in his gestures, perhaps because of the alcohol. People again commented on his painted nails and, although we had a general conversation about fashion and visual presentation, it was never linked to gender identity generally or Jess specifically.

When we went to bed Jess said he was glad we had had the party, that he needed to have it, to play host, which made me angry. He hadn't talked to me at all throughout the evening, nor had he touched me. Also, when his friend Harrison made fun of my voice, Jess had laughed.

9 December

Maybe because he realised how difficult the birthday party had been for me, Jess did something big last night. After dinner we

29

went up to the bedroom together and he showed me what he looked like femme. We were both so nervous. I don't think I have ever been so nervous.

A collection of thoughts chased each other in circles around my brain. I'm not going to like the way he looks. I'm going to react badly. I am going to ruin this moment.

I was overwhelmed by the trust he was placing in me by allowing me to really see him. I could only imagine how vulnerable he must have been feeling and it pulled at my heart.

It was the strangest experience. It was Jess, but not Jess. He was the same but different.

He had long hair that fell below his shoulders. It was loosely curled and completely transformed his face. He wore a simple t-shirt dress. Despite the nerves, there was an ease in his body. His gestures were delicate and playful.

We stayed that way for half an hour or so, talking on the bed. We didn't touch each other. He told me about trying out fake boobs made of stockings filled with rice, where he had got his clothes and underwear, what he hoped he could change about his face and his body, how uncomfortable he felt in his current body. I said I would teach him all about make-up and that we could play with all of my clothes and accessories.

It was strange when he took his hair off to go to bed. I had already got used to it.

We held each other until we fell asleep.

It's been a very big week.

12 December

I had my first psychologist appointment before work today. I arrived with ten minutes to spare so that I could fill out another very long form about my mood. It was quite a fancy office with lots of Scandi furniture, pot plants, natural light and magazines with titles like *Breathe* and *Living Mindfully*. The carpet was cloudy grey, though, which I thought was an odd decorating choice given the purpose of the business. It certainly wasn't helping my mood.

Susanne had worked at a counselling service at one point in her career, so I had asked her advice on choosing a psychologist. She told me that it was important to find one I felt comfortable with and that if I didn't like them I shouldn't hesitate in looking for someone else. She also suggested that, once I had a referral, I should visit the practice's website to look at the photos of the psychologists who work there to see who I was drawn to. I had completely forgotten to do this beforehand, so after booking my appointment I hastily checked the website for the 'Rachel' I was offered. She looked nice, about my age, and among other things she specialised in child psychology. I became paranoid that the receptionist had mistaken my voice for that of a child and feared that it was going to be a disaster.

Thankfully, Rachel was amazing and had no issue with my being an adult, so I won't have to trade her in for another psychologist. During our first session I just cried a lot and told her everything that had been going on. I'll go back again next week and we will figure out a more concrete plan of action. It was such a relief to finally talk to someone else and to be told that it is normal to be shocked and to grieve the loss of the relationship and the future I had imagined. She is also going to look for partner support groups and resources for me because I am still struggling on that front.

I told Rachel that the entire situation is complicated by Jess being on the autism spectrum. Normally that isn't much of an issue—I have a number of spectrum people in my life so I'm used to making allowances and adjustments—but Jess's difficulties with empathy, understanding and connection are really testing me at the moment. I don't have the energy to explain everything to him all the time, especially when I don't understand myself particularly well at the moment.

I also shared what we are starting to do about pronouns. It's definitely something I need to work on more. Since Jess said that he was non-binary we have been doing he/him for boy mode and they/them for girl mode/home time. Because we haven't told anyone else it can be hard for me to keep switching between pronouns depending on the mode and situation, but I guess it will become easier with practice.

All I want is for Jess to be happy and to feel comfortable and confident. I definitely think Rachel can help me sort myself out so that I can then help Jess achieve that.

I didn't feel like I could go straight to the office after my appointment because I was too exhausted from crying, so I went to Jess's work to tell him about my session, have a chai and rest. I should have just taken the whole day off, but oh well.

15 December

I have been doing my best to read as much as possible so that Jess doesn't have to educate me, as I have noticed that he often gets cranky if I ask him to explain something to me. Our conversation got heated yesterday when we were discussing trans representation in the media and I asked Jess to help me understand a particular comment. We ended up going home from work separately and I don't want that to happen again if I can avoid it.

I've also started to think more about what Jess's gender identity means for my sexuality. I find myself thinking a lot about how Jess looked femme that night. It still seems strange but also kind of exciting in a way. I did some googling and I think I could perhaps be pansexual, although I'm not entirely sure. I've never thought about my sexuality before and I got a bit overwhelmed by all the labels and options, so I gave up after half an hour or so.

Jess is going to start laser hair removal on his face and is thinking about hormones but is certain that he doesn't want surgery. We have been looking at photos of surgery results, which the old medical science student in me finds fascinating. Jess, however, is a bit squeamish and didn't handle it very well.

So much has happened so quickly, and Jess seems to change his mind, their mind, so regularly, it is hard to know what to expect and what decisions to prepare myself for. Maybe Jess will want surgery one day. I feel as though I am only just starting to adjust to seeing them in feminine clothes; the possibility of hormones seems too much—let alone surgery. Clothes and wigs feel safe; there is an impermanence to them. Hormones can't be taken off and put away.

I feel scared and uncomfortable but I also feel horrible for feeling that way. For putting my concerns and fears about changes to Jess's body and how I will react to them above their comfort and identity. Any time I have tried to raise any of that discomfort or uncertainty with Jess they have ended up being angry or disappointed in me. It seems I am not allowed to show any fragility; Jess seems to have the monopoly on that. They alone can be scared or unsure while I am expected to remain a monolith of strength and support.

At our session the other day Rachel said that it was natural to find this situation confronting. That I shouldn't beat myself up for not being instantly on board with such a big change. That it isn't possible to be strong all the time.

I just wish that Jess agreed with Rachel.

19 December

Jess has told me they are overwhelmed by the pressure of trying to navigate their identity as well as be in a relationship and they want more space.

They don't feel like they have the energy to be there for me; they just want to focus on themselves.

They say that I have always had their support whenever I needed it. Now they would like me to support them, to step up.

This somehow seems both reasonable and astonishingly unfair.

21 December

After many tears and conversations, we have agreed to get through Christmas and New Year and for Jess to spend more time femme over the break to see how we feel.

I have come up with a coping strategy: to keep my feelings to myself and remain as positive as possible.

I will be perfect.

TO: Jess

FROM: Me

Subject: Hello

Dearest,

I know we just said goodbye to each other, but my chest feels like it might burst so I just want to tell you that I think you are very pretty.

I enjoyed the days we spent together when you were femme so much and I am so grateful we had that time.

I must confess that at first I preferred you in boy mode, but over time I realised that was only because it was what I was most used to. Now I think we get along best when you are in girl mode. It makes me happy to see you more at ease. To see your sweet and playful side. To see you play with your long hair.

I think I'm just trying to say that I don't take any of this for granted. I don't take you for granted. You are an incredibly brave person and I admire you.

I'm sorry, this is probably overwhelming and too much.

I think you are beautiful.

THEM

22 November, six years earlier

'My mum has gone to visit my brother; would you like to sleep over?'
As soon as her mother had told her about the trip, the idea of having
him come over had intoxicated her.

'I would. I would like that very much.' He too had been thinking
of spending a night together and was relieved an easy opportunity
for them to do so had presented itself.

They were in the manager's office at work, taking a break.

'It has to be a secret sleepover, though. I don't think I'm ready
for my family to know about us yet.'

'How will you keep it a secret?'

'Well, Mumma will be away of course and my Dad isn't
around anymore and lives mostly overseas. Nanny and Poppy, my
mum's parents, live next door but I will just visit them so they don't
need to visit us. The only people who will know are the cats, but
that is fine.'

'I would prefer not to be a secret.'

'I'm sorry. I'll feel ready to tell them all soon. We are very close but we just aren't good at talking about personal things in my family. I would like you to sleep over if you feel comfortable, though.'

'I would still like to sleep over.'

The next night, after work, she drove them both home to her house. He had never been there before, but he recognised certain rooms from photos that had appeared in her text messages. The house was as he had expected: full of furniture, full of knick-knacks and full of cats. Her room was the same: an overwhelming display of who she was and what she valued.

As her bed was only a single, she had made up the double for them in her brother's old room. She was nervous. She hadn't been with anyone for years now. They sat on the bed together and began to kiss, gently at first and then with greater urgency.

'Are you sure you want to do this?' he asked.

'I do. I'm just nervous. I haven't had sex in a long time.'

'That's okay, I haven't either.'

They began to take off their clothes.

'I feel self-conscious about my breasts, is that okay?'

They were naked now.

'Of course. They're beautiful.'

He ran his hands over them and then down her back as she moved her hands along his thighs towards his penis, which remained flaccid.

'I'm sorry, I have trouble with that. I think I'm too nervous.'

'That's okay. Do you want to keep going or just go to sleep?'

'Sleep, I think.'

They kissed for a little longer and then climbed into bed. After turning out the light, they arranged themselves to face one another, their feet entwined. She could just make out the outline of his face in the dark and felt an urge to reach out and stroke it. After a little while he spoke.

'I used to be on medication for anxiety and depression when I was younger. Everything felt dull when I was on it—as if I were experiencing my emotions within a narrow range. It stopped the worst of my depression, but I could never feel happy either.'

'I'm sorry. That sounds very hard.'

'I didn't like the way it made me feel so I'm off it now. But I was on the medication for a long time—years. Since I met you, I'm starting to feel things again.'

She found his hand in the dark and squeezed it.

'I just want you to know that I'm not like other people.'

'I know that. There's nothing wrong with being different. I like that you aren't like other people.'

'Thank you, I'm glad.'

Eventually they fell asleep, but at some point during the night, she woke up suddenly, her vulva pulsing. The warmth of his body, the feel of his hand still within hers, had triggered a dream of their earlier fumblings. She shimmied herself closer and gently kissed him awake. He kissed her back and their hands began to travel over each other's bodies, their genitals pressed together.

The dark and their conversation seemed to have unlocked something within him because his penis was reassuringly erect. He reached for the condom and lube that hadn't been needed before and slipped them on. Suddenly, magically, he was inside her.

They didn't say anything out loud during or after, just cleaned up, slipped underwear on and climbed back into bed. She formed the big spoon around him and they fell asleep, both feeling rather pleased with themselves.

BUILD-UP

9 January

Jess is going to leave.

I lasted ten minutes at work this morning but I managed to sneak out before anyone else came in. Our office is on the top floor of the building and shares communal areas with three other organisations. The majority of my colleagues work in our main office in Sydney, with only the head of our research committee, one casual admin officer and myself currently working in this office. The chances of running into someone were quite low but I couldn't bear for anyone to see me. I quickly sent an email around to say I wasn't feeling well and would be taking the day off before escaping down the back stairs.

I am home alone now, crying properly.

Last night Jess went to see Harrison and told him everything. As they got ready to leave I asked them again to tell Harrison, hoping that this time they would. I waited all evening for Jess to come home, trying to imagine what might be happening at Harrison's house.

When Jess walked in the door, I was exactly where they left me, curled up on the couch. I could tell right away that something had happened.

Me: How was your night?

Jess: I told Harrison I am trans. I think I am trans. I'm actually trans.

This was the first time they had used the word out loud in relation to themselves and as they said it over and over I could see how elated they were. Jess then sank to their knees in the same spot they had stood when they first told me that they preferred to dress in women's clothes, in the space between the couch and the table, and began to cry uncontrollably. This was only the second time I had seen Jess cry and I wasn't entirely sure what to do.

After Jess had recovered they went on to describe how easy it was to tell Harrison about being trans compared to telling me about cross-dressing. Apparently Harrison reacted like it was nothing and this made Jess realise that it was too hard between us, that I wasn't coping well, that it wasn't working and that they really did want to leave.

We went to sleep in the same bed but didn't speak.

It's all so unfair. I am going to try to rest a little; I am making myself feel sick.

10 January

I've managed to convince Jess to stay for now, on the proviso that we transition into more of a friendship than a relationship. It turns out Jess had already asked Susanne if they could move back in with her. They didn't tell her what was really happening, just that we were having 'problems'.

While Jess and Harrison have been friends since they were young and even lived together for a time, their friendship is light and easy. They play games together and mostly talk about music and YouTube videos. They are as close as Jess can be with a friend; that is, they rely on each other only so far and share only so much.

I explained to Jess that it was spectacularly unfair to compare my reaction to them being trans to Harrison's. I am a partner. We live together. We have a sexual relationship. Harrison is a friend that they see once a month. Of course we would react differently. The stakes are completely different.

I also tried to explain again that this is something Jess has been wrestling with for decades whereas I've only had a few months to get up to speed. I should be allowed a period of adjustment. I shouldn't be punished for not reacting perfectly or being instantly accepting. We both know our home is the best place for Jess to play and experiment. They won't feel as comfortable doing that anywhere else. To leave now would set everything back.

Jess apologised and said it wasn't my fault, that of course I hadn't done anything wrong. That it is all them. They want to be better, to be the type of person they have always wanted to be.

To shed the things they don't like about themselves, especially their anger.

Now they won't come up to bed and are sleeping on the couch.

I feel as though I can never tell Jess the truth because it just sends them into a spiral of guilt. It's as though I have to protect them from themselves.

I've said that I will continue to support them, however they decide to move forward, and that we can just be friends while we figure it all out. I don't know if I can actually do either of those things, but I've committed to it now, so I'll have to try.

TO: Jess

FROM: Me

Subject: What I Need

Dear Jess,

I've written all this down for you as you asked. I hope it helps.

Things I need:

- To feel wanted, appreciated and valued.
- To feel secure in your affection.
- Physical contact and connection.
- To feel like I am being heard and that my feelings are valid and important.
- For you to communicate clearly with me. You rarely tell me how you actually feel, what you need, when I annoy you, how I can help you. This means I inevitably make things worse.
- To repair trust between us.
- For you to interact with the real me and not the version of me you have in your head.

Things I don't need:

- To feel like having to interact with me is a chore and something you have to endure and do out of obligation or charity.
- To feel incidental.
- Mixed messages. You encourage me to express my feelings instead of bottling things up, but when I do let myself go, you punish me for it. You tell me verbally that I can touch you, but when I do I can sense your revulsion.
- To be shut out.

Notes on depression from a podcast I was listening to. I thought this was relevant to how both of us behave.

- When in a period of depression he could make himself talk to the kids or take calls for work, but he couldn't speak to his wife when she checked in on him.
- He underestimated the impact this behaviour was having on her.
- He could manage to function when he was out and about but as soon as he was home he was miserable. It took her a long time to realise it wasn't her fault, it was just that she was the only person he felt able to express himself openly with, to show how he truly felt.

Being an empath:

Rachel told me that I am an empath, so I have been doing some reading about it. Hugh at work once told me that people on the spectrum often end up with empaths, which explains a lot about us.

Anyway, let's talk about all of this when we get home. Also, let's talk more about pronouns and time spent femme going forward so you can be as comfortable as possible.

Thank you.

11 January

We have just agreed that Jess will be femme all day tomorrow.

    I feel excited. It feels a bit like a date.

    I'll wear something cute, I think.

    Maybe my new dress.

    No, that's silly.

    I'll wear an old dress but new underwear.

    Yes, that will be good.

I wonder what Jess will wear?

    A dress hopefully.

    That would be nice.

    And sexy.

    I really want things to go well.

TO: Jess

FROM: Me

Subject: Today

You are sitting over at the table on your computer and I am on the couch. I'm not brave enough to say any of this out loud which is why I am writing to you.

I really enjoyed spending the whole day together femme.

I thought this afternoon was beautiful and it hurts that you regret what happened, especially when I was so happy about it.

As we talked and we cried I could feel that old spark between us. That magnetic pull.

I wanted you so much. To feel you inside me. To feel your lips, your hair falling against my face. To pull up your dress, to brush my hand along your thigh.

And then it happened. It all happened, just as I wanted. It was familiar, yet different. I can't even think of a superlative to do it justice.

After all these years, I feel like I am on the precipice of truly connecting with you. That there was some sort of veil between us before that has now been lifted. And now I seem to be falling more in love and I am finding it even harder to just be friends.

And as I feel more and more, you seem to be feeling less and less.

14 January

I can't focus.

I feel like if I could just talk to someone who isn't my psychologist it would help.

But I can't say anything.

It's been even worse since we had sex.

Which is confusing because I thought it was so lovely.

I haven't written any of the articles I was meant to.

I am not doing my best at normal work. I am scared they will notice.

I have to lie to people.

I hate lying.

The distance between myself and everyone else is growing.

I feel like I am losing myself in all the pretending.

Jess won't touch me again.

I did buy some bleach on my lunch break today.

Maybe we will try it on their arm hairs this evening.

Maybe it will help.

TO: Jess

FROM: Me

Subject: Things

Hello,

I want to get a few things off my chest.

I am finding it increasingly difficult to reconcile that the personal traits I am proud of, and which in any other circumstance would be considered positive—being generous, considerate and caring—are not considered positive when it comes to you. I struggle to either express or repress behaviours that come naturally to me according to what you need. I feel as though I am being selfish and that I need to make more of an effort to cater to your needs. I am trying, but maybe we could do better at meeting each other halfway?

I feel such an overwhelming pressure to be happy all the time and ignore any other feelings I might have. After a little while, the sadness I feel seeps out and we have a situation like last night. If I was allowed to be upset, and if we could actually talk about it, then I could feel it, let it go and be totally fine in only a little while. But the way things are currently playing out, I feel horrible nearly all of the time, which seems to make you angry.

I think because I don't have an outlet for my feelings I dwell on them and they appear much bigger than they really are. If I could communicate openly and honestly I don't think this would be the case. It would also help to validate and acknowledge my feelings and my experience as being real and important too.

Things I would like you to know:

1. I am sorry that I haven't been able to help you in the way you need so far. This situation has been confronting for me but with

the passage of time and a greater understanding of your thoughts, feelings and needs, I think I have been better at supporting you and can continue to improve.

2. I know it might not seem like it, but I do understand that the nature of our relationship has to change at this time. This is difficult for me but I will keep trying.

I want to say upfront that my motive for doing this is still romantic love. I know full well that you may never be able to love me that way again, and I do want what is best for you. If that is to keep me as a friend (with 'benefits', if you like) then that is something I want to give you.

3. I would like you to stay and I want us to keep working on a plan that makes us both comfortable. I still think our home is the best and most supportive place for you to play and experiment. I don't think you will have the freedom you need to explore in another space.

If you don't feel comfortable sharing a bed, we can set up a more permanent sleeping arrangement where you can get the rest and space that you need. This being said, you are always welcome in our bed whenever you want. I am also happy to sleep elsewhere if that is what is needed.

Bonus:

- I love you.
- I am proud of you.
- I am happy for you.
- I want you to stay.
- I will always be there for you.
- I am not going anywhere.

TO: Jess

FROM: Me

Subject: FW: What I Need

Hello again,

I also wanted to send you this again with added notes as it relates to my previous email.

When I first wrote this I was thinking of what I needed from someone who is important to me. My core basics. I would still want these things from my friends and my family, but in my email I did tailor them to you and perhaps I let my romantic love for you overshadow my intentions in creating this list.

I am sorry I wasn't clear enough about this when we discussed it the first time. It was not my intention for that list to drive us further apart. I had hoped that we would be able to work out what it was that we both needed from interactions with others and then identify where those things overlapped and where they didn't. I didn't and don't expect you to be able to fulfil all of my needs all the time. And I don't expect to be able to do the same for you. It's just not realistic. I do believe that these things still apply to our friendship and that in recognising and being mindful of each other's needs we still have the capacity to enrich each other's lives.

Things I need:

- To feel wanted, appreciated and valued.
- To feel secure in your affection.
  This doesn't necessarily mean romantic affection. Maybe affection is the wrong word. Maybe regard—or fondness, as you like to say—is more accurate. What I tried to say was that I don't want to have to second-guess whether you even like me as a person or not.

- Physical contact and connection.

  This still relates to a friendship. You may not be able to hug me or kiss me anymore, but if you can touch me like you did when you said goodbye this morning instead of not touching me at all as you did the day before, that would help me a lot. When you don't touch me at all, it affects me physically. My chest hurts and I can feel the space between us as if it is a heavy, grey cloud, which becomes overwhelming and unbearable. I think this is part of me being an empath.

- To feel like I am being heard and that my feelings are valid and important.

  I have felt a huge difference in this already. You have been acknowledging my experience and checking in with me.

- For you to communicate clearly with me. You rarely tell me how you actually feel, what you need, when I annoy you, how I can help you. This means I inevitably make things worse.

  It has helped me so much over the last few days when you have told me what you need. For example, when you told me that you didn't want me to speak and just wanted me to listen, or when you explained that you didn't want me to touch you.

- To repair trust between us.

  Again, I feel a difference with this already. You are being more open and honest.

- For you to interact with the real me and not the version of me you have in your head.

  I think this is something I have to help you with by being clearer about my feelings, but it will also help me if you tell me when you are unsure about something I have said or appear to be feeling.

Things I don't need:

I think working on the above things will stop me feeling the next few things. I think I felt those things as a result of a breakdown of communication between us.

- To feel like having to interact with me is a chore and something you have to endure and do out of obligation or charity.
- To feel incidental.
- Mixed messages. You encourage me to express my feelings instead of bottling things up, but when I do let myself go you punish me for it. You tell me verbally that I can touch you, but when I do I can sense your revulsion.
- To be shut out.
  I know this will always be difficult and I think we are doing a better job of this already, but I want you to know that I am realistic about this.

And now I had better get back to work because I haven't done anything actually work-related for a good hour now, which is very bad.

17 January

We went to work separately today.

I felt sick.

We ended up going home separately, too, because Jess was still upset.

I am upstairs now, hiding in my dressing room so that he can have some space. I am scared that Jess will want to leave again.

If things I did or my behaviour made him so angry, why didn't he say anything to me? Why didn't he give me the opportunity to stop or change?

I feel as though I have been so clear about this.

Maybe it isn't actually about me at all. Maybe he is determined to find fault with me in order to justify his treatment of me.

Sometimes I feel afraid of coming home, of opening the door, because I know things will be difficult and that he would prefer I wasn't there. Sometimes I feel as though everything I do annoys him, as if my mere presence is an unwanted invasion of his space and solitude. Sometimes I feel as though I am doing him a favour by going out or going away—or going upstairs, as I have now. That in removing myself I am doing him a kindness.

It is difficult to act naturally and it can be exhausting.

There seems to be no state of my being that is acceptable.

I try so hard to hold it all in, because I know he has enough to be going on with, that he doesn't need to comfort me on top of all that, but I feel like I am imploding. Actually, I feel as though I am on the verge of exploding; as though everything that I have tried to suppress, to hold in, is trying to burst out.

I feel like it is all my fault: that if only I was a better person, a different person, we wouldn't be in this situation. But maybe I never stood a chance. Maybe I can never succeed in this situation. Maybe Jess doesn't want me to succeed.

Sometimes I hate myself for still loving him and I hate myself for still wanting him to love me back.

If Jess does leave, how can I continue to live here in this house, where we built a life together? How can I even afford to stay here? Do we sell the house? Do I go back to Mumma's?

And I am crumbling. How could I let myself be destroyed by another person? I always thought I was better than that, that I had more self-respect. After what happened to me with my first love, I swore I would never let myself fall so deeply again. But I failed. I should have known that I can never do anything in half-measure. I love Jess completely.

And now it is happening again: a man in my life who has all the power, is dissolving the relationship on their terms and walking away with the outcome they chose, while I am once again left behind. Why do I let that happen? What is wrong with me?

I am the common denominator, it is my fault. The blame lies squarely with me.

Why can't I be someone who people want to stay with? What is wrong with me that no one can love me as I am?

I will always be alone.

I dread having to admit my failure as a woman and as a partner to my family and friends. What will they think of me? That I am weak and let myself be trampled on. They will pity me.

It would be easier if I could blame Jess and be angry with him, if I could cast myself as the victim of his moods, but I cannot deny the role I have played in my own undoing. If I can accept that the fault is mine, there is some hope that I can do something about it.

The only thing I want now is to go to sleep and not wake up. To drift away painlessly, so I no longer have to face this nightmare.

Despite everything, I still have a small pathetic hope that we might be able to work through this somehow, that we could start over, that he might be able to fall in love with me again, that I might be allowed to love him.

But maybe I am just in denial. Or maybe the thought of losing Jess is so painful that I am clutching at straws. Clutching at anything that means he isn't already lost to me.

Fuck. I forgot to use the correct pronouns. It is harder when I am upset or angry.

18 January

Last night we put on make-up together for the first time.

It had been such an awful day and I was feeling so low, I wanted to find a way for us to reconnect with one another. Jess was reluctant at first but eventually agreed.

After dinner we went upstairs to my dressing room. I sat Jess at my dressing table and pulled out everything we would need: brushes, primer, concealer, foundation, highlighter, blush, eyeshadow, liner, mascara. I put it on step by step, layer by layer, explaining what everything was for and how to apply it. We talked about the best ways to cover stubble, to soften the jaw. I told Jess that they could use shades that matched their natural colouring or just do what I often do, which is ignore the rules and put on whatever the hell I feel like. I did one eye in golden smoky tones and then encouraged Jess to do the other with my help so they could learn.

It was lovely to be so intimate with them, to be able to touch them and teach them.

When we were done, Jess went and put on their hair and we got out the polaroid and took a photo. I thought they looked beautiful and I told them so.

Afterwards we slept in the same bed and we snuggled.

21 January

A couple of months ago I booked a weekend away in the Southern Highlands for Jess's birthday. At the time I thought things between us might have improved and that some time away from the house would be a welcome escape. However, as the trip drew closer and things between us grew more fraught, Jess began to say that they did not want to go. I checked the terms and conditions, and while we could cancel I would lose my money. Besides, I had already told both our families that we would be going away, and as we still weren't telling anyone what was really going on I didn't know how to explain why we were suddenly cancelling our plans. I hoped they would change their mind.

The day leading up to the trip had been one of our most tumultuous and Jess became adamant that they wouldn't go. To save face with our families and to make the most of all the money I had already spent, I decided to go by myself and just pretend Jess was there. I would write and read and rest and take a break from the tension at home.

As I was packing to leave, Jess had a last-minute change of heart and decided to come. As much as I had tried to convince myself that spending the time alone was what I wanted, I was relieved. Jess hastily packed a bag, and we were on our way. They were fairly quiet on the drive up, but when we stopped for lunch in a small town they unfurled a little. After poking about in all the shops and buying a few sweet things we headed to the place I'd booked in fairly good moods.

We were staying in a Japanese-style studio on a larger property. It was surrounded by a peaceful garden with a pond and a fountain. A big lizard lived under one of the large mossy paving stones that led to the front door and frogs were croaking in the pond. The studio only had a double bed and was obviously made for romantic getaways. I suddenly felt worried that Jess might not want to sleep in the same bed as me, but they made no comment as I plugged my phone charger into my usual side of the bed.

We spent the next two days exploring the small towns of the region, shopping and eating. At one large second-hand store, Jess found an exquisite black vintage dress. We went into the change room together and I helped them put it on. It was an elegant cut, figure-hugging, with sheer back panels. It was hyper-feminine, an aspirational dress. We agreed that once Jess had breasts, and if they tucked, it would look incredible.

In the lead-up to our trip I had suggested to Jess that they might want to present femme all weekend, but what with the last-minute decision and scramble to actually come, they were in boy mode, which perhaps was for the best given how precarious their overall mood was. Only making purchases seemed to make them properly happy. In addition to the dress, Jess came across a book of poetry on gender and bodies completely by chance, which seemed serendipitous.

The bed was big enough that we could sleep without touching each other. We never kissed but sometimes we would hold hands. We talked until we went to sleep, reminiscing about when we first got together, talking about the transition and reflecting on how hard things were now.

Jess said that they wanted to tell Susanne about being trans when we got back, so we started making a plan. We decided to do it the next day, on their actual birthday, after dinner.

23 January

Jess was increasingly nervous, nauseous and irritable as the moment for them to reveal themself to Susanne arrived. There was no right thing for me to say, no comfort I could offer that seemed enough, so we both just struggled through as best we could.

Susanne and Alex were already seated when we arrived. We had such a lovely dinner but I couldn't quite enjoy it, knowing what was coming. We ate and drank, and I tried to behave naturally. On a trip to the bathroom I warned Susanne that Jess was finally going to tell her what was happening, but I didn't tell her what.

Susanne: I have about five ideas as to what it might be.
Me: You definitely won't have guessed this.

As we drove back to Susanne and Alex's house, Jess asked me to be quiet and not to say anything. The tension in the car was overwhelming; I could feel it crushing me. But I understood that this was something they had to do on their own.

I was sure that Susanne had warned Alex on their own ride home that something was up, yet by unspoken agreement we stuck to small talk when we first arrived, as if to put off the inevitable moment when everything would be revealed. After we gathered on the balcony, Jess asked Susanne and Alex not to speak, not to ask any questions, until they had finished what they needed to say. I could see how difficult it was for them, and I wanted so much to hold them, but I sat quietly in my corner. Jess tried to include me, but I let them speak because that was what they had asked me to do.

I could tell Susanne was in shock, but she was kind and supportive. When Jess indicated that they were open to discussing it, she asked lots of questions and so did Alex. Jess answered them all slowly and carefully, and promised to send some reading for them to do.

As the next day was a work day, and it was by now very late, we said goodbye and headed home. As soon as we were safely inside we stood in the entryway and held each other. Jess was surprised that they didn't feel more relieved.

Jess: I tried to include you, but you didn't say anything.

Me: You told me to stay quiet, so I did.

Jess: I just meant in the car on the way there.

I felt silly.

We went up to bed and continued to hold each other close. We talked about times in our relationship that we treasured. They kissed me. We hadn't kissed in such a long time, I could barely remember what it felt like. Soft lips, warm tongues. Jess told me they had forgotten what a good kisser I was.

They thanked me for being there for them.

24 January

Jess wanted to have a birthday dinner with Harrison, so I arranged to catch up with Belle. She is moving overseas soon, to New York with her partner, which is exciting for her but sad for me.

Belle used to be one of my colleagues but left about six months ago. I have only seen her socially a few times since then, partly because I was scared I would accidentally let slip something about Jess but mostly because I knew that without the distraction of work she would see through all my careful pretending instantly.

She knew I hadn't been myself for some time now and while I had hinted that something was going on she had no idea what it was.

Since telling Harrison and Susanne, Jess now felt comfortable with me talking to one of my friends, so that night, over dinner at her place, I told Belle the full story. Her partner was at football training and we had the place to ourselves. I felt I could be open and cry when I needed. It was such a relief.

After dinner we had tea on the couch, and I cried some more and we kept talking. It was comforting to have someone on my side, supporting me, understanding what I was going through, helping me to feel normal. A friend who knew and loved me, rather than someone whom I was paying to listen. Belle is the best and I am so lucky to have her.

When I got home I sent her a number of things to read. It is very strange to be in a position to educate others, especially when only a few months ago I knew so little myself. I really have come a long way.

28 January

Jess's oldest friend Lucas and his partner came over tonight. Jess cooked an elaborate dinner and told them everything. Much like with Harrison, it was a non-event.

Again I was compared to them, and again I failed.

9 February

A lot has been happening lately. Jess has got pretty new glasses, booked a consultation for laser hair removal and gone to the doctor for a mental health plan so that they can see a psychologist as well.

I am the same and have bought nothing new.

It seems like hormone therapy is back on the agenda, although Jess doesn't want to talk to me about it, probably because I was so scared the last time we discussed it. I have been doing a lot of my own reading on the subject because it still makes me nervous. Hormones have different effects on different people and there are health risks—but as Jess says, it is better to spend even a short time as a girl than a whole life as they are.

Jess is unhappy at work, unhappy within their body, unhappy with me. They are so unhappy and nothing I do seems to help. We tried to paint our nails together again. This time I painted Jess's and they painted mine. I suggested they paint mine slightly differently because my nails are so small and you would have thought it was the end of the world. I should have been more careful after the last nail incident; I should have known how sensitive Jess was about nails. I felt sick about it for hours afterwards.

I don't think Jess likes me anymore.

I don't think I like me anymore.

15 February

Belle's overseas move is now imminent and anything she can't take has to go. I had already done my part by buying most of her indoor plants, but with only two days left there were still plenty of things Belle had to find new homes for. As Belle and Jess were a similar height, she kindly asked me if Jess might like to go through the clothes she couldn't take.

I made the offer to Jess and they were moved that Belle would be so thoughtful. We dropped by her apartment after work the next day and while Belle and I talked about the logistics of her big move, Jess went through the clothes. They picked out a couple of loose floaty dresses, a sunhat and a blouse.

Jess didn't try them on while we were there but held on to them tightly until we left. At home, they tried each garment on, styling them in different ways, before packing them safely away for later.

18 February

After much deliberation, and with Jess's blessing, I decided to visit Harrison. I thought Harrison might need someone to talk to and I also wanted to make sure that he was in a position to support Jess. Jess has never been good at reaching out to their friends, especially when they need them, so I wanted to make sure Harrison understood how important this was.

That was my official agenda. My secret one was to create an opportunity to talk to Harrison privately so that I could share some of my side of the story. I wanted Harrison to know that I really was trying my best and that I still loved Jess.

I ended up having a surprisingly deep and meaningful conversation about work and life with Hugh before leaving the office, which meant I was hideously late catching the tram to Harrison's apartment. Harrison's partner Holly was out so it was just Harrison and me, and thankfully he is acquainted with my eternal tardiness. We settled in at the table.

He asked me how I was feeling and while I told him quite a lot—how shocked I was, how difficult it has been, how I am being compared unfavourably to him and to Lucas—I held back the worst of it. He is Jess's closest friend, after all, not mine, and I don't want him to think badly of Jess.

Harrison said he was also surprised when Jess told him and has found it confronting, but of course he wants Jess to be happy. He has agreed to make an effort to check in with Jess more often and to be more of a presence.

I didn't stay too long, as I wanted to have dinner with Jess. As I caught the tram home, two assumptions that Harrison had made kept niggling at me:

1. Now that Jess is seeking to transition into a woman, I mustn't want to be with them anymore because I like men.
2. If Jess transitions into a woman, they must now be interested in men.

I had thought about the first one before, but the second hadn't occurred to me. I never imagined that Jess might suddenly be into men. I had assumed that they would continue to be into me specifically and women in general and that the only thing changing was their gender expression.

It is curious how devoted we are to binary thinking, both in terms of gender and sexuality. Actually, not just binary thinking but *traditional* binary thinking. If you are a woman, you must be attracted to men. If you were initially attracted to men, you must always be attracted to them. We struggle with all of the in-between spaces, the grey areas that change. Anything that subverts the norm, really.

I have been lucky to have had many friends and acquaintances of different sexualities and gender expressions and maybe that has shaped my response to Jess questioning their gender. Perhaps I am more open to those in-between spaces.

TO: Jess
FROM: Me

Subject: This morning

Hello,

I have been thinking about why I was so upset this morning.

As I tried to explain, I can't decide whether you being asleep last night was a good thing or a bad thing.

You held me as we faced each other, our bodies pressed together, your head leaning on mine. When I turned around, you snuggled up to my back, hooked your legs into the crook of mine, and reached around to hold my hand. When you eventually moved away you kept your foot connected with mine like you used to.

At times I thought you were awake, which made me feel like you actively wanted to be close to me, and this made me feel safe and wanted. But now that I know you were asleep and have no memory of doing any of those things, it means your desire for closeness was subconscious. And that has left me confused. Does it mean that deep down you still have a desire for closeness that in time we can come back to in waking life? Or is our wakeful separateness the real truth and our nights merely a hangover from better days?

It's difficult to reconcile that a simple act of intimacy which has so much meaning for me is one that you have no awareness of participating in.

I have also been thinking about the impact the lack of intimacy and physical connection has been having on my self-esteem and body confidence. It doesn't matter how many times I tell myself that it's not about me, that it is about how you feel in your body, I can't seem to shake the feeling that there is something inherently unappealing about me and mine.

26 February

We had a difficult time this morning, but I have tried to clear the air with an email so that we can put all that aside, for the evening at least, to host the first book club of the year. We stopped in at the shops after work to pick up the snacks and then headed home to prepare.

Susanne was first to arrive, followed by Nora, my freelance writing pals Jana and Mia, and then Lucy. We would be missing Anna, who had recently moved to Melbourne, and Belle, who was now in New York. I had been strategic about the books I had selected for reading, in that they all had themes that could be discussed by everyone whether they had read the book or not. Our first book was about a woman who used prescription medication to induce a year-long sleep. Most of us had read it and we had quite a good discussion about depression, avoidance and the merits of different coping mechanisms.

Jess regularly talked about a desire to sleep all day and described bed as one of their only safe spaces. This coloured my reading of the book. Jess hadn't read it and so didn't raise any of their personal parallels. I didn't either, but after everyone had left and we were clearing up, I tried to raise my concerns about how Jess was coping. I told them I was worried about the long-term impact of continuing to repress, avoid and shut down, which caused a terrible disagreement. Well, we don't really have fights or disagreements. But we both got very upset. I've gone down to the couch this time to leave Jess the bed.

Every time I try to help it ends like this.
I mustn't be doing it right.

TO: **Jess**

FROM: **Me**

Subject: Today

Hello,

I hope you don't regret asking me to send this to you. I hadn't really intended to. It was more an exercise for myself to exorcise my feelings.

I had started writing this morning to get myself together so that I could focus at work. I was feeling a little angry and resentful after last night and so the first part is written from that headspace. I don't necessarily think or feel all these things when I am calm and more centred; they flare up when I am feeling emotional and then wind down when I can think and react more rationally.

This is from this morning:

> I am feeling worthless and meaningless.
> As though I am fading or turning into a shadow.
> Like I am hollow.
> Like I am dying an excruciatingly slow death.
> I have nothing to offer.
> I don't matter. In general or to Jess.
> This isn't enough.
> It isn't anything.

This is from after lunch:

> I still have such a fierce love for them.
> It burns in my chest.
> I can't imagine ending up apart.
> I definitely cannot imagine being with anyone else.

I can picture us together as two women.
Even when I feel angry with them, it just fizzles back into love.
The entire situation feels unjust.
I hate injustice.

This is me writing to you, just now:

I still want to keep trying to find a way forward.
If you will let me, that is.
And I don't mean to put pressure on you or force you to make the final decision. I mean that it is up to you to let me in, if and when you want to.
I realise I can't force you; all I can do is let you know that I will always be here, whenever you are ready.
You don't have to go through any of this alone.

2 March

Jess has left the house while presenting femme for the first time.

After they decided they were ready for this step, we made a plan. We settled on going to the movies as the best option because it would be dark and the other people would be focusing on the film and not on us. We were careful to choose a random afternoon session where we were unlikely to run into anyone we knew. Jess also thought that if we went straight there and back, and if they ate enough popcorn without drinking anything, they wouldn't need to use the toilet.

It took us an hour to get ready. Jess went through a number of different outfit choices before settling on one of Belle's dresses, a pair of my stockings and sneakers. We spent a lot of time on make-up and styling their hair. Jess didn't have a femme wallet or bag yet so I lent her a small evening purse of mine and I carried her keys and glasses case in my handbag.

We snapped a photo to send to Belle before we left. I checked the time difference; Belle would be asleep but would get a nice surprise when she woke up.

As we drove to the cinema we ran through scenarios, my stomach churning.

Jess: They will hear my man's voice and hate me.
Me: I can do all the talking if you prefer.

Jess: Someone might try to hurt me because I look hideous.
Me: I'll bop them with my handbag. And you look lovely.

Jess: I'll probably have to go to the bathroom.

Me: You might not have to.

Jess: Other women won't let me in.

Me: I'll come with you.

Jess: But they will tell me to leave.

Me: I'll tell them to fuck off.

Jess: What if we run into someone we know?

Me: We will cross that bridge when we come to it.

I found Jess's fear clarifying. I felt like there was finally a useful, practical thing I could do for them. I could be confident and assured. Or appear to be that way, at least.

Jess didn't feel comfortable with me touching them, so as we walked from the car to the cinema I was careful to keep my distance. I ordered our popcorn and we were quick to take our seats. It was difficult to focus on the movie, especially because I kept either sneaking looks at Jess or was suppressing the urge to reach for their hand.

As soon as the credits started to roll we got ourselves together and made a hasty exit. When we were safely at home, Jess declared the outing a success. We didn't see anyone we knew, no one spoke to us and we didn't use the bathroom.

15 August, five years earlier

They were on their way to Sydney.

After much discussion on her part and passive agreement on his, they had settled on the date of their first kiss to be their official anniversary.

She had booked two nights at a fancy hotel in the heart of the city while he had bought them tickets to a play and saved enough money for them to eat out. Together they had planned a visit to the art gallery, a trip to a bookshop they had heard about and lots of shopping in general.

They had taken the bus and, instead of reading the books they had packed, they talked about everything and nothing, regularly dissolving into peals of laughter or stealing kisses.

'I want you so much,' he told her, tracing a finger up her thigh.

'I want you too. Right now.'

But there was still two hours to go.

As soon as they checked into their hotel, they peeled off each other's clothes and had sex on the large, luxurious bed, their bags abandoned on the floor. They were hungry for each other, and their sex was rough, immediate. She grabbed his flesh and pulled him further into her as he kissed her breasts.

After releasing their passion, they re-dressed and unpacked before wandering out into the city in search of lunch. They remained in constant contact; stroking each other's arms, sneaking hands under the other's top.

That night, after an afternoon of shopping, a fancy dinner and the play, they climbed back into bed to once again entwine their bodies in sex.

'I love you, darling,' she breathed.

'I love you too.'

SUSPENSION

19 March

Rather incredibly, I have graduated from therapy. Jess and I had a really good week last week, so that may have contributed to my coming across as more optimistic and together than I actually am, but Rachel certainly thinks I can make do on my own for the moment and, now that I can talk more freely with Belle and Susanne, I think it could be true.

Plus I'll save some money, and more money is always a good thing.

24 March

Mumma and I are in Melbourne, packing up James's apartment. James is now spending more time overseas than not so it seemed silly to leave the apartment uninhabited. The three of us decided it was time to bring all of James's possessions home to Mumma's so that we could lease the apartment to someone else. It is strange being here without James but we have called him twice already. Once to tell him we found all his watches hidden under a chair in the bedroom and a second time to ask him why he hadn't cleaned out the spice cabinet before he left for the last time.

Mumma is having a post-cleaning nap and I am spying on the glampers holidaying in tents set up on the rooftop of the building opposite. A small child is whacking his sister with a stick and a glamorous old lady is reading on a sun lounger.

Yesterday, after a big day of packing and cleaning, I had dinner with Anna at her new place. It's really cute and in a fancy neighbourhood. She is settling in at her new job but is still homesick. We talked about books and our families and I told her all the hot goss from home. Then I told her about Jess and what had been going on.

It is much easier to talk about it all now that some time has passed and I have had a bit of practice, but I still cried. I felt the same relief and reassurance that I did when I first told Belle. I was reassured that I wasn't crazy, that I mattered, that I was important, that I was doing my best and that Jess was lucky to have me.

Tomorrow I'm going to tell my old friend from dancing, Timmy. We are meeting at her favourite Japanese breakfast place—the one next to the plant shop. Then we will go shopping and look at lovely things and be happy. And when I get home I'll tell my best school friend Nora. I'll do that over ice cream.

I'm really on a roll now but I still don't think I can tell Mumma. Neither of us are good at difficult conversations. I don't feel like I can bear her being sad or disappointed. Talking about what is going on with her is different to talking about it with my friends. Telling Mumma will make it all too real. She worries about me in a way no one else does and I don't want to upset her.

I am actually enjoying having a break from Jess.

9 April

I've upset Jess. I am not even sure how. It's about 11 a.m. now and they still haven't got out of bed. I've been up a couple of times to check on them, but they won't speak to me.

It's two in the afternoon now and Jess still won't get up and hasn't eaten anything. I took in some food at lunchtime but they haven't touched it. I am getting worried.

I've just messaged Susanne to ask her to come over after work to help us. I went up to tell Jess what I had done and about ten minutes later they came down and made a piece of toast and has been sitting on the couch waiting quietly for Susanne to arrive.

Susanne has gone home now. Jess behaved perfectly normally all through the visit and right up until bedtime. I still have no idea what any of this has been about but I seem to have been forgiven for whatever it was I did.

16 April

We had a nice moment today. Jess sent me a message asking me to remind them how to do a smoky eye. They had bought a beautiful new eyeshadow palette and wanted to put a look on while I was out to surprise me when I got home. I drew a picture of an eye on a little scrap of paper with instructions as to what shade to use where, took a photo and sent it back.

When I got home I told Jess they had done an amazing job and that they looked beautiful. I was even allowed to kiss them lightly on the lips.

27 April

Astonishingly I've only just realised that Jess and I seem to be stuck in a cycle. We have a number of good weeks, when we get along easily and naturally, when we are able to connect and make each other laugh, when we do lovely things together and talk and plan.

Then we have a horrible week in which everything is sickening and neither of us can say or do the right thing by the other and we sulk and hide.

When things are better between us I am more focused at work, I am a more attentive friend, I can do my freelance writing.

When things are bad, I am low, I am distracted, I have no energy. I feel like the weight of carrying both myself and Jess is crushing me.

In addition to that weight, I have been making myself as small as possible so as not to do anything that might make Jess leave.

It's a wonder I still exist.

Jess doesn't feel we need to write to each other anymore. I don't even feel like writing in my journal. My ability to keep it up has begun to slip away from me, but I'll persevere as best I can.

8 May

We had sex for the first time in months. Months and months.

I've missed it so much.

They were in boy mode, which was familiar and yet strange.

Overall it was a relief to have our bodies find one another.

Not to have to repress my urges.

But Jess couldn't kiss me. They couldn't look at me.

It was mechanical.

They were an empty shell.

So maybe I feel worse.

I'm not sure.

Maybe I won't think about it.

13 May

Mumma, Jess and I are on our way down to James's apartment for what feels like the billionth time to bring back the final load of his things.

Mumma is driving, I am in the passenger seat trying to write a review of a queer play I went to last night and Jess is reading in the back, not speaking to anyone.

Up until this morning Jess was all set to come with us, but half an hour before Mumma was due to arrive they changed their mind. I cried and pleaded desperately with them to change it back because Mumma had been so pleased when I told her that Jess was going to spend the long weekend with us, and I couldn't bear the prospect of having to invent some story to explain their sudden absence.

In the end they did come with us. I am going to be upbeat and not let their mood bring me down and hopefully that will help Jess thaw.

17 May

In classic fashion, after such a horrible start we ended up having a decent time.

On our first full day, we went to the beach to look around and have lunch. Jess was still closed off, so after we'd eaten I suggested that Mumma go back to the apartment while Jess and I went for a walk. We wandered through the park into the botanic gardens and after about half an hour or so Jess was visibly more relaxed.

The sun was hot and our feet were tired, so after a while we sat down by a pond and watched the people. Other couples, families. After we tired of looking at them, we noticed the most incredible thing. Two corellas were on the ground together, under a nearby tree. The tree was at the top of a slight incline, and one of the birds started to roll down the hill. When it reached the bottom it stood and waddled back up the incline to do it all again. Eventually the other bird joined in and they rolled together, all tangled. We had never seen birds behave like that before—it was amazing.

Jess and I left Mumma to her own devices that evening while we went to have dinner with Anna. I miss being able to have dinner together whenever we want. I miss having her at book club.

The next morning we met Timmy at the Japanese place for breakfast. Afterwards we went to the consignment store where Timmy works and Jess bought an amazing pair of Gucci sneakers and a super cute denim jacket. I bought a pair of Prada mules and a Harris tweed.

As well as cleaning and packing, we did everything you are supposed to on a weekend away: we went to bookstores, we spent too much money, and we caught up with friends. The drive home was much more pleasant than the one there.

Back in our own bed that night we reflected on the weekend.

Me: What was your favourite part of the trip?
Jess: Rolling bird. What was yours?
Me: Rolling bird.

29 May

Jess and Susanne went to a trans event together this afternoon. I wasn't invited. I'm trying not to be upset about that because it is important that they do things together.

While Jess has made connections with other trans people online, they haven't yet met anyone with a similar experience to them in person. Susanne had found a local community organisation that put on regular events and organised to take Jess.

When Jess got home I asked about it but they weren't really in the mood to talk. That night, though, as we lay together in bed facing each other, Jess told me that they worried that they couldn't connect with anyone. That they couldn't handle group situations. That they felt isolated in their experience.

Me: Don't worry, my love, you will find people like you. They are out there.

Jess: I don't think so. I have too many problems. I'm too broken.

Me: Don't say that.

We cried and I held them until they fell asleep.

14 June

Jess is still in a very bad place. I sent Susanne a message to let her know. She has suggested a new psychologist for them after the last one fizzled out. We talked about how difficult it is for Jess to find a psych they can open up to and then we bonded over Jess shutting us out.

Me: I am struggling. But Jess is struggling too.

Susanne: You poor things. Jess told me he worries about how much he is hurting you by being so difficult.

Me: I think I find it more difficult being shut out.

Susanne: Jess shut me out from the age of fourteen so I know what it's like to live with a ghost. It's hard.

Me: I do wish Jess would reach out to you.

Susanne: He is talking to me more often but not about anything deep. It's mainly strategies for moving forward.

Me: We cycle through the deep things, the practical things and nothing. It is hard. I'm sorry it's hard for you too.

Susanne: We both love Jess, we will always do what we can.

At least Susanne isn't on her own in supporting Jess anymore. We have each other.

24 July

We had the most glorious evening last night and I want to remember it forever. It was like a proper date. Well, it felt that way to me, at least.

Jess started a new job, so I suggested a celebration.

We got ready together, choosing our outfits, doing our make-up and hair. We ended up coordinating our looks. Jess wore a mustard skirt that had been mine and I wore a pea coat in the same colour. We took a photo together in my dressing room before we left. I liked that we matched. It made me emotional.

We caught the tram into town. People looked at us but there were no incidents. We had dinner at our favourite pasta place. I had the ravioli dish I always have and we shared garlic bread. I really like their garlic bread.

Jess was a little self-conscious, but on the whole I thought it was lovely.

As we left, the girl at the counter said: *Have a good night, ladies.* Jess was so happy.

Afterwards we went for a drink. I wanted to hold their hand, to kiss them, to be a couple. I got a little sad thinking about how I couldn't do that because we were supposed to be just friends. It rather put a damper on things.

We recovered by being a bit silly on the tram, and when we got home we had sex femme and it was beautiful. I really enjoy making Jess feel pretty. Being more delicate with them. Making them feel soft and feminine.

I think maybe this is what it is all for, all the pain and loneliness: the chance to be close to this beautiful creature and to help them become who they want to be.

27 July

Fresh off the back of our femme date success, Jess decided to go out and meet Harrison for dinner. I was nervous because this was the first time they had gone out femme without me. I sat on the bed as Jess got ready and I watched them walk off to the tram stop alone.

I asked Jess to text me when they had met up with Harrison safely in town, which they did. Apparently there was an incident, though, when one of the men who perpetually rides the tram had come up to Jess after drunkenly yelling at a few of the other passengers.

Man: Are you a boy or a girl?

Jess: I am neither.

Man: You do you, sweetheart.

And he stumbled off again. Jess said they were so terrified that their fist had been clenched around their keys in their pocket, ready to defend themselves.

I was on edge all evening at home. I couldn't settle to anything, I was too anxious, and kept checking my phone every five minutes. I tried to go to bed but I couldn't focus on my book.

At about 10.30 p.m. I texted Jess and asked if they wanted me to pick them up so they didn't have to catch the tram home alone. They didn't reply. I just lay there with the bedside light on, staring at the string of paper cranes Jess had made me that hung above our wardrobe.

However many agonising minutes later, Jess texted back to say it was all right, they were already on the tram. When I heard their key in the lock my body relaxed. They came up and started to undress and told me everything that happened. They had been scared, and people had looked at them, but ultimately it had been okay and Jess had felt good and right. They got into bed and we snuggled.

13 August

Today we finally went to couples counselling. It has been on the radar for some time but, what with one thing and another, we hadn't actually made it until now. The building was like a strange log cabin with small offices inside. Our counsellor, Rodney, was very nice and well-intentioned, but I am not convinced the session was helpful. We spent the whole time explaining the situation to him and not really doing anything practical. I had thought there might have been exercises to do or tips on conflict resolution or something like that. Rodney did make me a tea, though, which was something. Thank god it wasn't expensive.

We started by recalling how we had first met seven or eight years ago, when we were both working at the theatre and I was Jess's boss. Rodney asked what drew us to each other. I explained that I had been drawn to how quiet and shy they were, how when they spoke it was because they had something to say. We had connected over theatre, books, ideas. I felt like Jess was someone who could be silly and talk shit but who also had depth and substance. Jess was taller than me and slight with beautiful blue eyes and glasses. They were blond, which wasn't normally my thing, but the more I got to know them, the more irresistible

I found them. They definitely weren't like the other boys and I liked that.

Jess was drawn to my intellect and confidence, my bold personal style, my command of myself and others—all of which I already knew. The one thing I did learn from this exercise was that Jess had hoped that I, being a successful, together sort of person, could save them, a broken, lost sort of person.

I have been thinking a lot about this. I am not sure how I was supposed to save Jess without knowing that was what I was supposed to be doing. I am not even sure if that is a fair thing to ask another person to do for you.

On the whole, I didn't like couples counselling. I felt emotional and irrational in comparison to Jess's cool and logical manner. It was as though I was there to figure out how we could stay together but Jess was there to figure out how best to leave.

I was too upset to go to work afterwards so I called in sick. As I was sitting crying at home I remembered that one night—several months ago now—when, after we had turned out the light to go to sleep, Jess had reached out to hold me and told me that they would never leave me.

They were a toxic, damaged person, Jess said, and as much as they loved me they would always hurt me and would never have the strength to leave me. If it ever got too much for me, I would have to be the one to leave. They told me the story of a philosopher—I can't remember which one—who destroyed his wife, and Jess said they didn't want to be that person.

I said I would never leave, that Jess *wasn't* that person, that we were just struggling through something bigger than us and I understood that.

18 August

It was our six-year anniversary during the week. The day itself was disappointingly normal. We had dinner at home.

However we both took Friday off work to spend our customary long weekend away in Sydney. We decided to catch the bus so we wouldn't have to mess around with parking. We did all our favourite things. The gallery. Our favourite bookshop. A play. The latest fashion exhibition. Hot chocolate in the park. Window shopping. Eating.

I had asked Jess if they wanted to spend the weekend in girl mode, but they said no.

Overall it was a sad weekend. I felt as though I had a permanent lump in my throat and tears burning at the corners of my eyes. I had a horrible feeling that each thing we did was probably for the last time.

On the second night, as we cuddled in bed, I tried to explain how I felt about my body. That I have been conditioned my whole life to strive to be thinner, smoother, stronger. That when I am out and about in the world, on social media, talking with friends, I face a constant background pressure to change my physicality to match the ideal. That I used to be able to deal with that because I was well and I knew it was stupid and I came home to an environment where I felt safe and loved and appreciated. I came home to a loving partner who enjoyed my body, who took pleasure in it.

Now I face all the usual pressure and scrutiny but come home to an environment where I am not welcome, where my physical presence is completely unacknowledged. This has manifested in a loss of my body confidence and an increasingly inescapable feeling that I have become unattractive or unappealing and that is why Jess doesn't want to touch me.

Anyway, I feel like I said it much better at the time but that was the gist.

Jess said they were very, very sorry and it wasn't me at all. That it is their unhappiness within their current body that makes it difficult for them to interact with mine. That I had the physicality of a Renaissance muse and should be off riding a clam somewhere. That not to be drawn to such a body said more about the beholder than the beheld.

I thought that was kind and it helped a little.

25 August

We had proper sex tonight. Jess had ordered some lingerie for themselves as a surprise present for me. They looked incredible in it. I don't think I will ever forget how absolutely incredible they looked.

I dressed up sexy too, but felt lumpy in comparison. I tried not to think about it.

I waited in the dressing room with my eyes closed as instructed while Jess got everything ready. They then came to get me, leading me into our bedroom.

Each time we have sex now I wonder if it will be the last time. I also wonder if I will be able to live with that particular experience being the last time. Sometimes, during the night, Jess tries to have sex with me in their sleep and I let them. When they wake up and realise what they are doing, abruptly stopping in apparent disgust, I turn over and cry silently.

But this experience was beautiful and special and I won't have to try to forget what happened.

Except that Jess still couldn't kiss me. They did try but couldn't, which killed me. But I kept going.

28 August

I've been thinking again about being pansexual. I cannot stop picturing Jess in their lingerie, and I have been increasingly turned on by Jess's femininity.

I've spent the best part of the evening googling various types of sexuality and pansexual is still the closest thing I can find to how I feel. However, the more I googled and the more I read, the more I felt like it didn't actually matter to me. I think it has been very important to Jess to be able to put a name to how they feel, to give shape to their identity, to find a community of people like them, and this makes absolute sense. But I am not so sure I need that. I don't know that I need to define this aspect of my identity.

So after all that googling, I am just going to fantasise about femme Jess in their lingerie and leave it at that for now.

1 September

A very exciting thing has happened.

This afternoon, a big brown rat was sitting inside the bowl of birdseed, gorging itself, its long tail hanging over the edge.

When I was doing my honours year at university I had to work with mice. I must have killed almost fifty of them in the course of my immunology work, the poor things. When I was running an experiment I would walk over to the mouse house with my little esky in hand and inject my mice to get their immune systems going. Then I would return in the afternoon to kill them and collect their spleens to take back to the lab. Working with them was always sad and confronting but I made sure to be kind to each mouse and would talk to them and stroke them so they were less afraid.

Jess thought they had seen a mouse the other day but, as it had gone by so fast, weren't entirely sure. We continued to keep an eye out for it, more for something non-transition-related to talk about than out of genuine interest, but as we stood together to watch our new friend eat birdseed, I knew it was a rat. I remembered being jealous of the neurology students who had got to work with rats. These rats had been glossy and white and seemed much more exciting than my little mice. I think it will be interesting to observe my new rat; to feed it and love it and not have to kill it.

8 September

Nanny is in hospital. She is dying of the flu but is in denial.

The other day Mumma called me at 4.30 a.m. because Nanny had fallen over and she needed help getting up. I came over to help and we still couldn't get her up, so I just called the ambulance, not realising they had been fighting about calling for it before I came.

The person on the phone thought I was a small child.

Operator: Is your mum there to help you?
Me: She is but I am a grown woman, this is just my voice.

The ambulance came and they used an impressive machine to hoist Nanny up and it turned out she really was deathly ill, so they had to take her away. We repacked her hospital bag with more sensible things, got Poppy ready and followed them in.

Nanny spent the day and night in intensive care and is now in a ward. She keeps insisting that nothing is wrong with her and that she wants to go home, and we keep explaining to her that if she doesn't eat or drink something soon she won't be going anywhere. Poppy is usually the sick one and I don't think he likes all the attention being on Nanny, so he keeps talking loudly about his various ailments to anyone who comes in.

It's likely Nanny will be in hospital for a week, so it's going to be draining.

I wish Jess would comfort me, but they are too wrapped up in their own problems.

I just don't know if I can cope with much more.

23 September

Jess told me again last night that they want to leave.

I think they really mean it this time.

It's been a year since Jess first told me that they feel more comfortable in women's clothes. One year and a couple of days to be exact.

I didn't bring it up with Jess at the time. I just noted it in my diary and then thought about it all day at work.

I wonder what would have happened if I had never said anything about the hairs?

Would Jess still be hiding their true self?

Would we be unhappy?

Who would we be?

Who would I be?

24 September

We have agreed to spend some nights apart. Jess had come home to pack some things up to go stay with Susanne, but I had a panic attack, so they ended up staying with me. I've never had a panic attack before. It was horrible. I couldn't breathe and my chest hurt.

I tried to sleep in our bed but I couldn't. I just cried and felt sick and like I wanted to scream and throw things. I've never felt that way before. I wanted to die to make it all stop because it didn't feel possible to contain myself within my body.

I tried to sleep on the floor of the dressing room but that was also unbearable, so eventually I came downstairs and Jess let me sleep on the couch with them and they held me while I cried myself to sleep. It was just like the first night we moved in and had to sleep on the couch because we had no bed except no one was crying then.

TO: Jess

FROM: Me

Subject: Planning

Hello,

If this really is it, there are some things to work through and we need to sit down and do it properly.

Talking points:

- What do you want a relationship between us to look like going forward?
- Do you still want this to be your home? Do you want to have occasional sleepovers? Do you want to leave things here? Do you want to come here every day and then just sleep somewhere else?
- What about sex? If we wanted it, could we still have it?
- Is there a possibility of being together again one day?
- Financially, you need to stay until December. I propose you live here part-time till the end of the year and then we can re-evaluate.
- I acknowledge that we aren't good for each other at the moment and that there is work to be done that needs to be done independently. What I resist is the assumption that this work needs to be done in complete isolation. Can we help each other? Provide space and support?
- Can we still be each other's favourite person? Each other's first point of contact?
- Does it have to be defined at all? Does it have to look like something that already exists? Can we create what we want a relationship between us to look like?

My desires:

- For you to be happy. To feel confident. To feel secure. To feel independent.
- For me to be happy. To feel good about myself and my abilities. To be confident and kinder and more forgiving.
- For us to one day find a way to be together that allows us both to be happy.

Also:

- I've realised that I get trapped in negative thought spirals. This makes me look at everything differently, which then impacts those around me and, being a people-pleaser, the moment I realise my spiral is impacting others, it fuels the spiral further. It then becomes hard to recognise what is a normal way of feeling and what is a catastrophised way of feeling, what is reasonable and what is not. I often need other people or something external to turn those negative thoughts around. I need others to convince me that I am worth something, that I am a good person, a successful person. It would help if you could say positive things to me sometimes. I know I need to learn how to do that for myself, but it does help to hear it from you.

28 September

Last night I slept alone in our house for the first time.

We have lived here for nearly three years now and I have never had to do that before.

It was always me who went away. Jess never went anywhere.

I used to fantasise about what I would do if I was left alone in the house.

It certainly wasn't crying until I nearly vomited.

29 September

We have just been over to Mumma's to tell her that Jess will be going to stay with Susanne for a while.

I have hated pretending that everything is the same as always between us, but I didn't want to worry her. It was a relief to be more honest and I was glad that Jess agreed to come with me. I was expecting them to back out and leave me to tell Mumma on my own.

We downplayed everything but I could tell Mumma was upset and confused. I cried a little. Jess was stoic.

I am going to fill her in about the gender stuff in bits and pieces over time, but we have made a good start. I made the decision to tell her in a more gradual fashion because I think she will find it confronting otherwise.

I also don't want her to think badly of Jess for treating me poorly.

30 September

We went back to couples counselling today and thank goodness I had the foresight to take the whole day off work. I've been sitting on the couch since we got home watching our rat go about her business in the backyard while trying to get myself back together.

It was even worse than last time. Or maybe it was the same and my ability to cope has decreased. Either way, it was absolutely awful and I've said I won't go back again. Jess is still using it as an opportunity to exit the relationship in 'the best way possible' while I am still secretly hoping that there will be some sort of miracle.

I don't want to think about it right now and I don't even feel bad about repressing it.

I really, really hate couples counselling.

2 October

It doesn't look like Jess is going to stay until December.

I have spent the last hour putting together budgets based on various scenarios, ranging from Jess still contributing some money to Jess contributing no money at all.

It's quite bad.

I can cover the mortgage, bills and household expenses etc. on my income alone, but I won't be able to make any credit card payments and will have virtually no spending money. Which is terrible because I love spending money. I think I'll have to use my savings to pay down my debts, but that will leave me with next to no safety net.

Jess says that I can have the house and all the furniture, which on the face of it appears a kind gesture, but I am now thinking they might be getting the better end of the deal. I may have all the assets, but I also carry all the risk. And the emotional burden of remaining in our house with all our possessions while Jess walks away with their whole income to start afresh.

I wish I hadn't spent $1500 on those antique embroideries on our anniversary trip. That seems a very ill-advised purchase in hindsight. Maybe they will appreciate in value. Not that I would sell them, of course.

I certainly won't be selling any of my clothes or shoes.

Anyway, this is absolutely fucked.

9 October

Jess slept over last night. We had agreed they would sleep over every few days but that hasn't really been happening. After so much time apart, last night felt like too much pressure. We were strained and awkward with each other. Every topic felt either too big or too mundane given what was happening.

I find I am growing to resent our house. I can't bear being in it, but as soon as I leave I burst into tears and want to go home again. One day I made it all the way to the office before I lost it and had to turn straight back around. I have noticed that if I have arranged to meet Hugh I will usually be able to make it, because the fear of letting him down by not turning up trumps my fear of breaking down outside the house.

Yesterday I confessed to him that Jess had left. Normally after we have lunch together, Hugh reads the papers and has a nap on the couch while I go back to work, but on this occasion when he came back after his relaxation time I wasn't working, I was crying. It's a relief to have told him, really, because now he can look out for me at work. Hugh told me to take time off when I need it, to work from home if that's easier, and to try to take care of myself. Him being so nice and understanding made me cry even more and I am determined not to let him or my other colleagues down.

I absolutely cannot lose my job, so I just have to keep getting up, going to work and trying my best.

TO: **Jess**

FROM: **Me**

Subject: Hello

Hello,

It's been a while. Only a little while since we have seen each other but a longer while since we have written.

It is odd spending so much time alone in the house. I don't like it. It gives me way too much time to think. I've been picturing you spending time in a new room, in a different house. I can't believe that I used to fantasise about you going away so that I could be here alone.

If I am completely honest with myself, which I am trying to be, I know that you have not been good for me. You continue to say it and I have continued to deny it. I think I hear you now.

You have always kept me at a distance, never letting me close enough to really see you. Even with that distance, I knew I had come closer than anyone and that made me feel special. Perhaps I perceived being allowed to come the closest as love. Regardless, things have been unequal for a long time now, even before your transition. I have been giving too much and you have been giving too little.

We really were happy, though. You were kind, you would kiss me, touch me, do little things for me, we would laugh. Holding on to those memories, memories of love, happiness and partnership, has kept me going while things have been difficult and uncertain. They are what I had hoped we might come back to one day if I hung on long enough.

You say that I am wonderful, that you still care for me, that I haven't done anything wrong, but you have left me—prefer to spend time apart and to leave our home. If I was negatively impacted by this relationship before, it's nothing compared to what I feel now you have left. The withdrawal of your affection and attention has only affirmed and cemented the negative feelings I was experiencing regarding my self-worth, body and sexuality while you were still here.

I've realised through this time alone that I do want a partner. I want someone to share my life with. Someone to love and support me. I want to feel needed. I want equality. I want to feel like I give value to someone and for them to give value back. I want someone who doesn't just take from me and then leave.

I want that person to be you.

13 October

I finally did something I have been putting off for weeks. I cleaned out the shed and fixed things so Mrs Rat can never come back. It was incredibly traumatic and is by far one of the most horrible things that I have ever done.

She had somehow got into the shed and every time I opened the door I could hear her scrambling about, to the point that I was too afraid to look. I enjoyed watching her when she was out and about in the garden, eating, carrying leaves, being cute, but the prospect of encountering her in such a confined space disturbed me. It was unnatural. Also, it was starting to smell and I needed her out.

I opened both of the shed doors, put on gloves and a face mask and started pulling things from the shed one by one and hosing them down. After going through two large tubs I called Mumma. She didn't think she could help but offered to come over for moral support. I told her not to worry and I kept going. After pulling out a few more things I discovered the rat's nest. She had stripped pieces off an old astroturf offcut that was at the back of the shed and placed them inside a large cooking pot along with shreds of old shopping bags. It was full of fur and shit.

At that point I started to cry so I called Jess to see if they would come and help me, but they were buying furniture for their new room at Susanne's so I didn't end up asking. To their credit, Jess realised I was in distress and did offer to come, but I knew I wouldn't be able to handle it, not on top of kicking out Mrs Rat. I knew I would behave badly now that I'd found out they were buying furniture and would probably end up causing a scene, so I said no, thank you, and hung up.

I kept cleaning, pulling things out, hosing them off. I had to throw a lot of things away as they were too ripped and rat-shitty. When I got to the very back corner I discovered my rat had been in the shed the whole time and was now hiding on one of the shelves. I had been making so much noise I hadn't heard her, but there was no mistaking her scrambling and squeaking now. I got the hose, adjusted the nozzle to jet and started spraying everything left on the shelves.

Mrs Rat sprang from her hiding place and ran for a small hole in the top left corner below the roof line. I came out of the shed and trained the hose on her as she ran along the fence and jumped down. I started to scream but kept spraying her until she found a new hidey-hole in the garden. I turned off the hose and I could hear her making the most pitiful noise, like she was crying.

I quickly cleaned out the rest of the shed but now my crying was mixed with her crying and I felt awful for putting this poor rat, who had just wanted a safe, warm home, through so much trauma. I blocked the entrance hole to the shed with a glass jar, closed it and hid from her for the rest of the day.

14 October

Mrs Rat has built a new makeshift nest on the ground between the shed and fence overnight. She has brought over a whole pile of tanbark from the garden and used it to block the entrance.

I'll give us one more day to recover from what happened and then I'll have to move her on from there too. While I was at Mumma's picking up some bricks to block up various other holes, she told me I had been too soft with the rat and that it is well and truly time to stand firm. The last thing I need is rat babies.

Jess and I were texting in the afternoon and at first it was harmless enough, as I was giving a rat update, but then things got serious and they said:

I'm not sure if I ever really loved you. I don't think I know how
to give or accept love.

I think that is the cruellest thing they have ever said.

15 October

I can't sleep. I'm too angry.

Jess gets to wake up knowing that he did the right thing and that he is on the right path. I wake up every day feeling further and further away from the life I was trying to build. I'm no longer even on a path.

He has all the power because I am the one in love. No matter what, I lose out.

He keeps saying he is doing what is best for us. That also seems unfair. I don't think he should get to decide what's best for us or what's best for me. He is doing what's best for him.

It just makes him feel better to think his actions are benefiting me in some way.

Doing what's best for us implies I had some say or choice in the matter. That it was a shared decision. That we were both involved.

What's best for me is not an option.

This isn't the life I chose. I feel like it's been thrust upon me and now it's up to me to make something of this horrible situation. A consolation life. If I am still unhappy then it is my fault because I failed to reshape my life in some way or to see this as some sort of opportunity.

Fuck. Fucking pronouns.

Even after everything they have done, they still get to be the good person because they are trying to help me. I can't be angry at them because they are trying. So I still can't express my feelings. My anger feels unjustified. I can't let them know how absolutely shit they are sometimes because if I do they will retract the help they have been offering.

I just have to suffer quietly and accept what they are offering, because even if it isn't what I want, it's better than nothing.

17 October

Although my brain was telling me I should, I decided not to cancel book club. Of all the regular attendees, only Susanne and Nora knew that Jess had left. I didn't think I could face telling the others yet, so I asked Susanne to make sure she and Jess arrived early, and thankfully they did.

We were discussing a collection of feminist essays that only Mia, Lucy and I had read. Everyone ate and drank and talked and laughed, and it was just like old times until everyone started going home. Jana's car had been written off after someone crashed into her the other week so she asked if someone could give her a lift. Jana lived quite close to Susanne, which would have given the game away, but thankfully Nora saved me by jumping in with an offer even though it was out of her way.

When everyone else had gone home, Jess helped me clean up before leaving with Susanne.

They really don't live here anymore.

26 December, three years earlier

During her lunch break, on the last day of work for the year, she picked up the keys to their new home. It was the ultimate Christmas present, a two-bedroom townhouse about twenty minutes from the city.

Technically it was her house; her parents had given her some money towards the initial deposit over a year ago, on the proviso that it would be purchased in her name only. But as the townhouse was being built, and they saved for the remaining deposit together, she only ever referred to it as 'their' house.

On the day the keys were picked up, he had almost finished packing. His mother would also be leaving their shared rental home to move in with her own partner. He was anxious about moving away from his mother and apprehensive of being in constant proximity to her, his partner.

'Are you sure moving in together is the right thing to do?' he had asked her.

'Of course! We will have our own space where we can arrange all of our books, knick-knacks and clothes exactly as we want. And we can have sex wherever and whenever we like.'

He felt as though he were merely a passenger swept along by the current of her excitement. It wasn't her fault; a part of him did want the life she described but he was also paralysed by a fear he couldn't name.

On Christmas eve they dropped off the first few boxes of their personal possessions and on boxing day, both of their mothers helped them move the big things in: their new couch, the furniture they had bought at IKEA, their second-hand fridge and washing machine. The bed-frame, mattress and curtains they had painstakingly chosen wouldn't be arriving until the new year.

That night, when they were alone, they ordered pizza. They sat together on the floor, nestled between their boxes, eating and planning the unpacking and furniture-building efforts of the following day. After discovering that neither of them had packed toothpaste, they prepared for sleep by transforming their couch into a makeshift bed and repurposing the cardboard boxes containing their new bookshelves as makeshift curtains.

As they lay down, their bodies naturally found each other, fitting together like puzzle pieces. This was it, she thought. They had gone all in. Their finances were intermingled, they were building a home together, they were beginning a life as partners.

'Are you excited, my love?' she asked.

After a little while, he answered, 'I really am.'

AFTER

23 October

My hair has been falling out and has blocked the shower drain.
I was having a big cry in there this morning when I finally noticed
that water was pooling around my ankles. I turned the stream off
but the water wouldn't drain away. It's been there all day, soapy
and accusatory. I stopped in at the supermarket on the way home
from work and bought a large container of chemicals to unblock it.

TO: **Jess**

FROM: **Me**

Subject: Friday

Hello,

I think you will be gone by the time I get home. I doubt I would have
been able to say this in person anyway.

Your callousness and selfishness the other night floored me.

You are asking me to do an almost impossible thing on an
impossible time schedule. You are asking me to let go of over six years
of love and turn it into a casual friendship at a speed that suits you
and makes you comfortable. And you had the gall to turn that around
on me and try and make it my fault for not adjusting fast enough and
accepting what you are offering.

At first you suggested a transition. At first we agreed that you would
sleep over twice a week. This happened once before it got too difficult
for you. We then agreed to see each other a few evenings a week,
which is also now too much for you.

Again, you are asking me to go from seeing you every day, from
living a life together, to first one thing and then another depending on
what you can handle.

If a few hours a week to help me transition out of our relationship
is too tiring for you, I want to once again remind you that I live in our
house, surrounded by our things. I can't go one minute without being
reminded of you, of us, of the future I wanted.

My ability to look after myself, to cook and clean, means nothing. It
is representative of nothing. If I can't do those things right now, that's
fine. I'm devastated. I am allowed to not have the energy to do menial
household shit. Also, even if I could function on that level it wouldn't be
indicative of what I'm feeling on the inside.

Relying on someone is part of being in a partnership, in a relationship. It's part of caring about someone. The fact that I rely on you and need you is not a flaw. There is nothing wrong with it. I don't think I rely on you in a way that is abnormal or unreasonable. How dare you say that the people you need in your life are those who don't rely on you for anything and only want to see you every now and then, and that if I can't fit that description then too bad for me?

The fact that I keep trying to do these impossible things, to give you space, to fit around your schedule, is testament to the depth of my feelings for you. This is what I wanted to tell you the other night. Despite my not being your biggest fan right now, the longer this goes on the more sure I am that I love you and that you are my person. You said you disagreed before I even finished. You might have meant that I am not your person, but if you were disagreeing with my assertion that you are mine, how dare you presume to tell me how I feel?

I want to be your friend but you are being entirely unreasonable in your expectations and demands of me.

27 October

When I got home from work today the last of Jess's things were gone. All of the anger I had unleashed in my email drained away as I walked from room to room, opening and closing drawers and cupboards, taking in the empty spaces.

The finality of so many intimate objects being removed was so shocking I was beyond tears, which in itself was a new feeling. The empty bookshelf in particular killed me. When we first moved in we had spent days on those shelves, organising our books by genre, arranging the knick-knacks around them just so.

Materially, Jess had taken so little—clothes, books, laptops, a games console, toiletries—it would take only half a day of rearranging to make it appear as though Jess had never lived here. In overall impact, however, the emptiness they have left behind is so vast it threatens to swallow me. Their imprint is everywhere. Their usual chair at the table. Their favourite water glass. The toothbrush they accidentally left behind.

I'm glad I wasn't here to see Jess pack everything up. It would have been too much.

4 November

Jess used to make jokes about the things I would miss about them when they were gone. It was often irritating things, like kicking me out of the kitchen when they were cooking or holding me down and making horrific faux-eating noises in my ears.

I do miss those things, but with all this time alone I am finding the things I miss most are much nicer.

It's opening the door and having them look up to greet me from the couch.

It's talking before we go to sleep, our faces close.

It's seeing our favourite bird in the garden and admiring it together.

It's having dinner made for me.

It's Jess using the sesame seed grinder I bought them even though they think it's pointless, and putting the box it came in on the shelf because it's pretty.

It's letting me come grocery shopping even though I'm annoying.

It's coming to events with me even though Jess hates them.

It's them copyediting something I wrote even though it's bedtime.

It's watching films and TV shows together and discussing them.

It's putting the toothpaste on my toothbrush and insisting that I floss my teeth but then letting me have the night off when I'm too tired.

It's being silly and laughing so hard together our stomachs hurt.

It's letting me pop an irresistible blackhead on their forehead even though they really hate it when I do that.

It's kissing me tenderly on my forehead.

It's tucking their arms inside the sleeves of my top when they hug me so our skin touches.

It's waiting for me to be safely inside the car before they get in.

It's looking at me like I am the most important person in the whole world.

It's nothing big or grand. It's just a series of small, intimate moments and gestures that made our life together what it was.

It's everything.

9 November

I had lunch with Susanne today. We went to a cafe near my old high school. I had forgotten how much it looks like an old cabaret hall. All red leather with moody lighting and a wooden stage.

We hadn't seen each other since Jess left. She had called me a little while ago to say that she hoped I didn't think she had abandoned me, that she needed to help Jess while they were in crisis mode. I had mostly just cried and said I understood.

At lunch today we talked about everything. Again, I cried quite a bit. It's been so hard for Susanne to lose the son she thought she had, to gain a daughter she doesn't yet know. To lose the daughter-in-law she loved, who she could see was so good for her son.

I told her how I have been crying every day, sometimes for hours, how I am dehydrated from crying so much, how I feel exhausted and hopeless. She told me about something that happened to her when she was my age and helped me to see that I am unwell and that I need to get help.

I had to run straight back to work afterwards so I feel as though I have forgotten a lot of what we talked about, but it was a very important conversation and I am so glad we have each other. I am going to go to the doctor and ask about medication and I am going to go back to the psychologist.

Since I got home I've been thinking about how Jess was always so good at reading me. I never felt as though I was able to read them as well. I did know them better than anyone, and I felt pride in that, but I was not allowed to see them fully.

I always thought that was down to some flaw in me; that I wasn't loving or observant enough. But now I realise it was actually that Jess was withholding so much, both from themself as well as from Susanne and me. It wasn't that I was self-centred or an uncaring partner. It wasn't a flaw in me; it was that Jess was so good at acting a part.

Susanne never saw any of this coming either, and I take comfort in that too.

12 November

I think I tried to commit suicide today.

It was very strange.

I stayed home in the morning and tried to do some work but couldn't really focus, so after lunch I thought I would go into the office to see if I could do any better in there. I couldn't face having a shower, so I just put some clothes on, packed up a few things and walked out to the tram.

I wasn't feeling very well; I was kind of spacey. But I often feel that way these days, so I just kept going. I was standing on the platform, waiting. There were other people around.

It was like I was me, but I wasn't. Like I was talking to myself as well as listening to someone else.

The tram is coming.

Why don't you step out in front of it?

It would be easy.

You would feel so relieved.

It would be nice.

You should do it.

And then the tram came, and I found myself stepping out in front of it. I didn't mean to, it wasn't something I had actively decided to do, it just kind of happened and I couldn't stop it.

But then someone yelled out and the conversation in my head was interrupted and I stepped back.

I got on the tram because I didn't really know what else to do. My whole body was throbbing. My heart was pounding and my ears were ringing. Tears were pouring down my face. No one spoke to me, so I just found a seat and rode the tram all the way into town.

I went straight into my office and closed the door. I texted Susanne and told her what had happened. She said she would come and check on me after work.

I didn't really know what to do, so I just caught the tram home again and lay on the couch until Susanne arrived.

I am not going to tell Jess.

I am definitely not going to tell Mumma; she would be too worried.

13 November

Today has been a horrific day.

I went to the doctor in the morning and filled out a mental health questionnaire. The results were very, very bad.

I talked about my crying but I was vague about my suicide incident. I don't why; I just couldn't say it out loud. It's a miracle I managed to tell Susanne about it yesterday. The doctor has prescribed antidepressants. I have to build up the dose gradually and they will take about two weeks to kick in. I also got a new mental health plan so I can go back to my psychologist.

Jess asked me if I would like to go to trivia with them, Susanne and Alex at the club that night. Because I was feeling slightly more optimistic about my situation after going to the doctor, I said yes. It was something the four of us used to do together all the time. We would have dinner, catch up on what was happening in our lives and try our best to beat all the other teams at trivia.

Since Jess left, we have gone a few times, and on each occasion Jess came to pick me up so that we could still arrive at the club together, like a couple. Tonight, however, although Jess offered to pick me up, they said they would have Susanne and Alex in the car with them. They said it didn't make sense to travel in separate cars from the same house. I was disappointed, because if the three of them came together there would be no chance of Jess and me spending any time together after trivia. I tried to change Jess's mind, but they wouldn't budge.

I stood out the front and watched as Jess pulled up in our old car. I climbed into the back seat. Alex was sitting in the front, in the middle of relating some anecdote, and Susanne was in the back, laughing. They were a unit, and I was the odd one out. Jess didn't even turn around to say hello to me. I could feel tears pricking at my eyes and my throat closing over. I wanted to get out of the car, to run back inside.

When we got to the club, Jess tried to talk to me, but it had been such a bad start to the evening I couldn't really recover. I hadn't seen Jess for days, and I was upset from my tram incident and the dire depression score on my mental health test. There was so much to say, but I didn't feel like it was safe for me to say any of it. Plus, Susanne and Alex were behaving like it was any other trivia night and we were still a happy family.

It got worse and worse throughout the evening. We were awful at trivia and our rival team was revelling in our poor performance.

At the end of the night, they dropped me home. As we pulled into our driveway and I realised I was going to have to get out of the car alone, that Jess wouldn't be saying a proper goodbye, that the three of them were going to drive away together to another house, I completely lost it. I burst into tears and, without saying anything to anyone, I got out of the car as quickly as possible and ran inside.

I cried for a good hour then went to bed.

I am never, ever doing that again.

19 November

I had to do some hardcore googling but I finally found Rachel again. She had left her previous practice and now has her own. It was so nice to see her again.

I gave her all my paperwork and told her about my meds. I spent our time together bringing her up to date on everything that has happened. I didn't mention my suicide-ish incident until right at the end of the session. I know she is exactly the person I should be talking to about it, but I was too ashamed. I want her to think I'm better than I am—which is very stupid and completely counterproductive.

She observed that I didn't seem too concerned about it. And while I did downplay it a little, it's true that I am feeling less worried about the whole episode now that I have had some space from it and more time to think.

I realised that given my medical science background I have naturally been considering my current mental state in more of a chemical context. I think of my suicidal thoughts as symptoms of my poor depleted brain rather than a conscious behaviour or choice, and I find that quite soothing. I am not necessarily going out of my way to hurt myself; I'm more of a symptomatic opportunist.

But perhaps that is scarier, because I now need to avoid potential opportunities in case I take action. I need to think about that more, actually.

Rachel and I talked about my brain offering suicide to me as a solution to a problem, as a means of relieving my pain and giving my exhausted mind and body a break.

Like, should I:

a) See Jess?
b) Not see Jess?
c) Sell all the furniture?
d) Move out of our house?
e) Commit suicide?

It's not really what I imagined being suicidal would feel like, but it makes sense to me. I am going to keep an eye on things, and once my meds kick in, this suicidal ideation should disappear. There are other steps we can take if they don't, like referring me to a psychiatrist, changing my medication or suicide watch. I find that reassuring.

3 December

Jess and I have just had a very good week. At times it was as if nothing had changed. We laughed, we hugged, we were less self-conscious. We talked about everything: the big things, the little things. We put up the Christmas tree and watched trash movies. The transition has overshadowed everything, has overtaken every aspect of our lives, but for a few brief moments it almost felt as though we were through it and everything was as it should be. We were two ladies enjoying each other's company.

Jess cooked for us, just like they used to. They don't like the kitchen at Susanne and Alex's place; it is small and pokey. They miss our fancy new kitchen with all our beautiful kitchen things. It seems so silly that I have them all because I can't cook. The kitchen is one of my most hated areas now.

On one of the nights Jess came over we left at the same time because I was going to have ice cream with Nora. We said goodbye at the letterboxes, standing a few feet apart. I told Jess I loved them—it just burst out of me before I could stop it—but they came over and hugged me and told me they loved me too. I started crying, and Jess was worried they had made me sad, so I explained that I was happy. I cried all the way to picking up Nora because their words had meant so much to me.

Maybe I am not so crazy after all.

Was it pretend before? Or is it pretend now? Have they been saying they don't love me in order to protect me?

I think they do still love me.

I think they are trying to protect me.

It's my birthday soon, but this year I feel no obligation to do anything, which is a relief as I am in no fit state for anything or anyone. But I do wish Jess would sleep over. I don't want to wake up alone on the actual day.

Maybe they would.

Maybe I'll ask.

TO: Jess
FROM: Me

Subject: The good week

Hello,

After our good week your recent coldness and distance has felt more confusing and difficult to bear. We are back to the old cycle.

I have been keeping notes in my journal. I had intended to come back and flesh them out properly but, what with my depression, I haven't had the strength, so I can only offer these dot points.

Following our good week:

- Easy, communicative, emojis, I felt like my companionship was sought and enjoyed.
- I felt optimistic and hopeful, less crazy.
- Asking them to stay the night came off the back of that optimism. After what happened by the letterboxes I thought they might say yes. It was a mistake. I pushed them too hard. I wasn't as resilient as I thought. The rejection was crushing. I thought I would be able to handle it but I could not.
- This came from a fear of not wanting to be alone on my birthday—a day that is important to me and one I wanted to share with the person I care about.
- I'd asked multiple times in different ways. I hadn't explicitly said, 'I need you.' But I had said that I didn't want to be alone; I had admitted that I was scared. I wasn't sure how else to say it. They weren't picking up on it.
- Eventually I was explicit and they did come. And they baked me a lovely cake. I've been eating it for dinner each night.
- I felt like I had to beg.

After my birthday:

- It has been a week since we've seen each other. Multiple plans have fallen through.
- I've been disappointed in how things have played out.
- They are shut off again, not reaching out, not communicating, polite but distant. No emojis. No chitchat.
- The ease has vanished and I feel as though I can't talk to them. I feel like a stranger.
- I've felt a cooling towards them. A hardening. I feel disappointed in myself.
- I want them to reach out to me, but when they don't I find myself having to ask. Then, when they do come over, it is clearly out of a sense of obligation and I end up resenting them.
- In being the person to reach out I am also the one to sit with the rejection. I'm tired of the constant rejection.
- At what point do I acknowledge that I'm doing this to myself? That this is one-sided, that they have nothing to give me and that I need to let go?

Thank you for texting me. Thank you for still wanting to understand me. I do hope this helps.

TO: Jess

FROM: Me

Subject: RE: RE: The good week

I think it is unfair of you to say that I am dependent on you. It is natural to resist letting go of someone who is important to you. You are twisting my love into a weakness, a fault. You conflate it with feelings that you project onto me.

I've said this before, but we have gone from seeing each other every day, from sharing everything, to a 'friendly distance', as you call it. I don't want friendly distance. As I have tried to convey to you, my feelings haven't changed, they have only strengthened, although I wish this wasn't the case.

I don't think you will ever be brave enough to actually say that you don't want to have anything to do with me anymore. You skirt around the edges, sending mixed messages, trying to spare me pain. But what you are doing is cruel and misleading.

I cannot continue to subject myself to the excruciating torture of friendly distance.

P.S. I appreciate what you say of my kindness and my writing. I still feel a fool even if I express it well.

16 December

Susanne came over to check up on me and she told me I had to let go of my hope. She said that I would never move forward as long as I held on to it. I find this so hard to acknowledge. A lot of the time my hope feels justified and reasonable. At other times I feel as though I have gone mad and am delusional.

I don't mean to make things so complicated and to be so difficult. I feel beyond my own control most of the time. I am so stuck in my head and I can't seem to stop myself from doing or saying destructive things. I know that everything would be easier if I could let go of my love and accept a friendship. Instead, I feel a strange combination of pride and shame that I can't put my love for Jess aside.

I think a lot about what loving someone means and believe that the truest display of my love for Jess would be to let them go. I feel ashamed that my selfish desire for connection stands in the way of that action. I sense myself coming close to letting them go but I don't seem to be able to do it just yet.

19 December

I am feeling lower than I ever have. It's a sickness, a heavy weight that drags me further and further into the abyss. The prospect of not seeing Jess at all scares and sickens me. The possibility of being forgotten, of being erased along with Jess's male identity, of not being needed or wanted, of Jess being better off without me, is corrosive.

I am losing so much—my partner, my best friend, my wellbeing and potentially my home. I don't think I am strong enough to survive it. I could have borne any one of those losses if I hadn't lost Jess as well.

I am back to crying every day now. The initial reprieve afforded by my medication has worn off.

I think Jess should let me go for their own good. They have a chance to be a better person, to be happy.

I can't find either of those things now.

TO: Jess

FROM: Me

Subject: RE: A plan

Hello,

You were right. I haven't been well. You mentioned in your email
that you would feel better if you knew I had some sort of plan.

I wouldn't say I have a plan, but these notes I took to my therapy
session feel like the scaffold of one. It's as close as I've got.

Big questions from the session:

- When do I move forward?
- What does that look like?
- What role should Jess play?
- What if I am fundamentally changed? (More withdrawn, less
  ambitious, not able to connect with anyone intimately.) How do
  I adjust to a different version of myself?

Things to do before the next session:

- Decide what to do about Jess.
- Assert some control, set clear boundaries.
- Attempt to rebuild trust in myself. Think of ways to do this.
- Actually let the publications I have been contributing to know that
  I can't write for them at the moment instead of ignoring their emails.
- Think of ways to reclaim the things in my life that were mine.

Longer-term things to work on:

- Coping with grief—I read somewhere that grief is love with no outlet.
  I am struggling with having no outlet or a reduced outlet for the love

that is still flowing out of me. Rachel suggested that a pet might
fill that gap.

- Trying not to interpret all of this as my fault and an indication
  that there is something wrong with me—seeking fault is a way of
  asserting control. If something is my fault, I can work on it to make it
  better. If Jess didn't leave because of me, there is nothing I can do,
  and the injustice of it is overwhelming.

I hope that helps you feel better.

TO: Jess

FROM: Me

Subject: <none>

Hello,

I finally changed the sheets yesterday. Mumma had done hers the day before and when I said that I hadn't changed them since you left she told me that was disgusting. Then, after a moment, she realised why I hadn't changed them and she cried. Well, I think she did.

I carefully constructed my 'fake you' under the doona this time; it's as if you might be sleeping with your head tucked between the pillows. Sometimes I wake up during the night and I find myself clinging on to you.

I ended up having breakfast with Lucy after that. I was running very late and I had to speed walk. I haven't walked that fast in months. She was very kind and said that she had been worried about me. She thought it could be good that you and I took a break from one another. She said I should focus on giving to, and looking after, myself for a change. Lucy is so wise.

Whenever I talk to anyone about what is happening they are always surprised that I am still so supportive of you. A few colleagues came down from Sydney for an informal Christmas party the other day and Cameron asked me if I thought I could still be with you after your transition. I said yes. She said that was amazing and that I was very special. I find it strange when people say things like that to me because I don't feel special or amazing; I'm just doing what feels natural and right to me. I think I am horrible most of the time.

Today I went into the office to water my plants. I was feeling lonely so I went into the shared kitchen and sat down with some people from one of the adjacent offices. We somehow got to talking about pumpkin pie and I said that you made me a pumpkin pie every year. We also talked about mulled wine and mead. I told them about the time at the old house where we warmed up that bottle of mead in the microwave and got quite tipsy and laughed and were silly. I didn't cry telling the stories, but my heart felt like it was being squeezed tight.

I don't know if you will text me tonight. I hope you do. I am too scared to text you first. After seeing you last night and that going well, I found your texts today to be quite distant. It was jarring. When you hugged me and kissed my forehead it was blissful. I never wanted it to end. I smelled of you afterwards and I went to sleep holding my shirt.

Which is rather pathetic.

You said that you cannot be my solution. I'm not sure that I want you to be my solution, I just want you to be open to perhaps wanting me one day. I think I would feel better and be able to do anything if there was some chance. Maybe that does mean I want you to be a solution. Or part of one. When you said that you have been vowing to never love again, I felt both comfort and fear. It makes me think that even if by some chance you did come to feel for me again you wouldn't act on it for fear of hurting me. But I was secretly glad that you wouldn't love someone else.

I know that sounds selfish.

I really do want you to be happy. You deserve to be happy. You are kind and brave and so lovely. I have a horrible feeling I have become one of those guys in movies who just tries to bully the other person until they love them. I'm bullying you and I know I am bullying you, but I can't stop. I feel awful about it and I am sorry.

25 December

James couldn't come home for Christmas, so it was just Mumma, Nanny and Poppy, the cats and me, which meant it was like most other days except for presents and too much food. Mumma and I explained away Jess's absence by saying they had to spend Christmas with their family *and* Alex's this year.

Mumma and I had breakfast together before unwrapping presents. We called James to show him each of the cats begrudgingly wearing their Christmas collars. Mummy and I went over to Nanny and Poppy's for lunch where we ate far too much too quickly. We left Nanny and Poppy to nap and went back home to digest and watch a silly Christmas movie. After I had recovered I went on a long walk to Nora's for an afternoon visit before coming back for dinner and another silly movie.

When I eventually got home, I discovered that Mrs Rat had given me the gift of four tiny rat babies, which is just what I always wanted.

TO: Jess

FROM: Me

Subject: Yesterday

Hello,

I am glad we got to see each other last night. Thank you for having a little Christmas with me.

I have been thinking about something you said, about you striving to make peace with everything that has happened and, through that process, to shed the bad from within you. As I thought about that, this phrase came to me:

I am a casualty of your quest for self-exploration.

I wrote it down, but I haven't thought much more about it. It makes me feel a little sick for some reason.

I want to shed the bad from me too. I don't think I have handled things well and this experience has exacerbated my negative character traits. I want to be loving and understanding but I find myself often being selfish and resentful. I don't like myself very much right now.

Anyway, I don't know if any of this is helpful or reasonable, but these are my thoughts for today.

TO: Jess

FROM: Me

Subject: RE: RE: Yesterday

I don't even know what to say in response to that.

28 December

Jess texted me with an 'x' at the end, so I sent a nice response back. They didn't reply again. I hoped they would. I then checked my emails and they had sent a clarification to their previous email and it was horrible. I felt embarrassed about being so nice in my text message. The email was so short and straightforward. Accusatory. I've cried and cried and cried.

I suppose it hurts so much because of course it's true.

They say I keep talking in circles and I need to look to the simple answer. Well, the simple answer is this: I am not simple and none of this is simple.

This is what I know:

The person I love doesn't love me anymore and has left me.

The person I love only wants to see me once a week as a friend.

The person I love finds it hard to spend time with me because it makes them feel bad.

The person I love couldn't touch me. The person I love couldn't kiss me. If we had sex they could only do it from behind.

I'm grieving the loss of my relationship, my closest friend and the future I was working towards. I have been left behind in the home we built together, surrounded by our things.

I am clinically depressed. I am not coping. I am becoming a worse person.

The person I love treated me poorly for a long time and I let them.

They are sure they were right to leave.

I continue to love them and desperately try to convince them to love me back. I am no longer the type of person they could actually love.

I pretend to my grandparents that we are still together. I pretend to my mother that things aren't as bad as they really are. I pretend to acquaintances that we are still together because it's too painful to explain. I haven't told my father anything.

I cry every day, often for hours.

I sometimes contemplate suicide.

I am ashamed of myself.

I'm scared I won't recover.

I'm scared I'll waste my life.

I'm scared I won't achieve the things I could have. That I'll never be able to be in a relationship again. I'm afraid of letting myself be close to others.

I hate my body.

I try to convince myself that they aren't a bad person.

I can't confront what loving a bad person indicates about me.

I try to convince myself that I can be better. That I didn't deserve this. That I can understand them and that they can understand me.

I still love them and fantasise about them.

I am deranged.

I am crazy.

I am unreasonable and irrational.

I am unlovable.

Pathetic.

I have no self-respect.

So maybe there is actually a simple answer and it goes like this: They don't love me anymore.

The sooner I accept it the better it will be for everyone.

29 December

I've got myself back together for the most part. I am on a higher dose of medication now and that is definitely helping me bounce back better from more extreme episodes.

I need to keep reminding myself that Jess sees things in a different way from me; they process them differently. Being rational and logical, looking for the simple answer, comes more naturally to them. I am led by my emotions and instincts, especially in times of great distress.

I have always admired those traits in Jess, and when I was well we complemented each other perfectly. But now that I am unwell and trying to contain and process more than my fragile heart can handle, their logic and reason feels like an affront.

I booked my flights to visit James today. I think it will be good for me to have something to look forward to. I'll fly into London in early May to do all my favourite things before meeting James in Paris. I was disappointed to have missed him when I was in Europe last, but thankfully this time he will be in the one place long enough for us to catch up properly. We have been talking a lot more lately and it will be nice to see each other in person.

Maybe Jess will stay over while I am away and water the plants.

31 December

Susanne and Alex are throwing their famous New Year's Eve party tonight.

I planned to have a lovely dinner with Nora before going over to Mumma's.

I told Nora over Thai food and an extremely elaborate mocktail that Jess had invited me to the party but that I didn't think I should go. She didn't think I should either.

I drove past anyway on my way to Mumma's. The fences are low and I could see them all gathered out the back. I pulled in behind Jess's car. To see it there, at home in a different driveway, made me feel sick. Before I could get too nervous I quickly got out of the car. I got as far as the doorstep. I stopped and listened to the voices, clutching my bag.

I thought I heard Jess. Tears had already started leaking from my eyes and I still felt nauseous, so I went back to the car and texted Jess to say I couldn't do it, I couldn't come in. They replied instantly saying they understood and wished me a happy new year. They didn't know I was just outside. After sitting and crying for a few moments I left. I could see Jess and Susanne through the kitchen window as I drove away.

I cried all the way to Mumma's. When I got there I sat in the car for a little while and pulled myself together before going in. I didn't tell her what I'd done. We watched a murder mystery and drank ginger beer.

Then I went home and went to bed before the fireworks even started.

TO: Jess
FROM: Me

Subject: <none>

I'm sorry about what happened this afternoon. I had hoped I could be more normal and that we could have dinner. I felt so nervous about seeing you.

When I saw you all the time, it was easier, it wasn't a big deal. Now, when meetings are a week apart, I have so much love bursting from me that it is difficult to contain it all in those small moments when we do see each other, and I can't act naturally.

That's why it all goes wrong. And then I have to wait an entire week to try again, and by then I have had a whole new build-up. It was better for me when we saw each other two or three times a week, which is what happened that last good week. There is less pressure on any one occasion.

Your physical presence still has such a visceral impact on me. The less time we spend together, the harder it seems to be when I do see you. I stare at you more, I want to touch you more, I am more attuned to your energy and your presence. I know it makes you uncomfortable and I am very sorry.

I'm sorry I kissed your neck. It was an impulse, a reflex. I don't think there is any way I can relate to you or express myself that doesn't cause you pain.

It's been horrible to start a new year without you. I think of you spending time with your mum and Alex, playing games, reading. I've been doing all the things I like to do, but being alone—not being able to tell you my little bits of news, to hug you on the way to the kitchen, to be silly together—is killing me.

It's not that being on my own is bad (it's just that there is too much alone time) or that the things I do for myself have less meaning (I would have done them anyway), it was just better and nicer when I was doing those things alongside you.

I was cleaning out my bedside cabinet yesterday and going through all my precious things, and in an act of masochism decided to read every card you have ever sent me. The card that touched me most was the one from our very first anniversary. You wrote:

> My dearest darling,
> Every day I spend with you brings me one step closer to becoming a complete person.
> Happy Anniversary, I love you.
>
> xxxxxx
> Forever yours,
> Jess

I'll always treasure those words. All I've ever wanted is to help you feel whole and happy.

TO: **Jess**

FROM: **Me**

Subject: RE: RE: \<none\>

I think something within me finally snapped when I read your response.

To continue to group me with Harrison or Lucas as a 'closest friend' does a disservice to our relationship and what it was. I should have realised that when you kept getting angry at me for not reacting like Harrison or Lucas, you had already started to think of me differently.

I am not fucking Harrison or Lucas. I never have been and I never will be. I am someone who loved you, who was your partner, who built a home with you. Who bleached your arm hairs for you, who taught you to put on make-up, who helped you to feel good in your body and made you feel sexy, who told you that you looked beautiful. Don't you dare devalue what I offered you and liken it to what they do. And that is not to demean their friendship; I know it is important. But it is not the same. I did not offer so much of myself as a partner and a lover to be remembered or thought of as any less. I would never and will never do that.

I don't know that I will ever forgive you for leaving right when you started to be your true self. Damn you for only doing the fucking work now that you have left and I won't get to experience the goddamn benefit. And damn you for saying that offering me meagre points of connection is exhausting when I offered you unrelenting support at my own expense, despite being broken and exhausted for over a year. I am so unbelievably angry with you.

Yet even though I'm so furious and disappointed, I still love you and believe in you. I think that love and belief gives greater fire to my feelings. I cannot accept that this is the type of person you are. You are better than this.

I'm sorry, but I cannot reach out to you anymore.

If you ever want to, you can reach out to me. I will be here. You can ask me to do anything and I will do it. I will always love you and want to be close to you. I mean this.

I have to accept that you may never reach out to me again and that is something I will have to live with. I hope with my whole heart that this won't be the case.

I do not intend to contact you again. I am going to give you the space to become who you want to be.

I really do hope that one day there will be a place for me in your life.

Goodbye.

TO: Jess

FROM: Me

Subject: RE: RE: <none>

I am immensely relieved that you wrote all that.

I want you to be honest with me and tell me how you feel.

I want you to speak your heart and mind.

That's all I've ever wanted.

I think I am going crazy because you haven't been.

I want you to challenge me, to stand up to me.

All I have heard is people telling me how kind and generous and amazing I am.

I want to know that I am being horrible and selfish.

ME

21 January, five years earlier

She had booked a surprise trip for his birthday; it would be their first weekend away together. He knew flights had been booked but not where to, although he had his suspicions. Her brother was overseas and his apartment in Melbourne was empty. The day before they were due to leave she revealed the surprise and the countdown began.

The next morning her family drove them to the airport. She thought he seemed anxious so, after they'd said their goodbyes, she took charge, directing him through security and into the departures area.

'Nanny has given me airport money,' she told him. 'Do you want to spend it now or save it for later?'

'What's airport money?'

'You know, spending money for the airport. Sometimes I spend it on snacks, or a magazine, or a cup of tea. But maybe we should save it to buy something when we get there.'

'Whatever you think.' He hadn't been to an airport in years, and his grandparents lived too far away to give him airport money.

They hung around the gate until their flight was called. Once they had joined the growing line of other passengers waiting to board, she bounced around him, kissing him every now and then as they moved up the queue.

'We are going to have the best time. I'm so excited!'

'I am too.' It wasn't a lie exactly, but he did wish he could manage his anxiety better.

They ended up with a whole row to themselves. As the plane took off he closed his eyes tight and she reached across to hold his hand. She hoped they would have a good time. She wanted so much to make him feel special on his birthday.

They caught a transit bus from the airport to the city before walking from the station towards her brother's apartment. She made this trip to Melbourne three or four times a year; he hadn't been here since he was a teenager. As they wandered along, she pointed out various landmarks, cultural and personal. They planned all the things they would do.

It was midday, so after dropping off their luggage they had lunch at one of her brother's favourite cafes before an afternoon tour of bookshops. They found a couple of books each in the secret bookshop upstairs, and at an antique bookseller tucked away beside a church they found a collection of old maps. He chose a map with bold lines that traced the shape of an erect penis and bought it as a birthday present to himself.

It was only his birthday eve, so they had a quiet dinner at a nearby pizza place before setting up the sofa bed to watch a movie. As they lay together, their feet touching, half focusing on what they were watching, half focusing on each other, she suddenly felt overwhelmed.

'Can I tell you something?'

'Of course.'

'I love you.' It was the first time she had said it out loud and as she did she realised she had felt that way for some time now.

'Really?'

'I do. Is that all right?'

'It is. I don't know if I'm ready to say it back yet. I'm not sure if I know what it means to love or what it even feels like. I'm sorry.'

'It's okay, I'm not upset. I just wanted to tell you how I felt.' And she wasn't, really; she knew he cared about her and would express it in his own way in his own time.

'Happy birthday eve.'

'Happy birthday eve.'

NOW

9 January

Intentions

1. To get through the day
2. To take my journal seriously
3. To go into the office
4. To have dinner with Jess
5. To find out about hormones
6. To talk about everything sensibly

Happenings

I listened to an episode of one of my favourite podcasts this morning on the way into the office. A guest was speaking about abandoning a friend who was struggling with substance abuse. The friend, a charismatic, indomitable character, had been revealed to be something quite different, someone frail and disappointing. The guest had begun to withdraw his friendship because he wasn't friends with *that* sort of person. His friendship circle was made up of the old sort: colourful, together, normal.

The guest speaker said that incident had made him reflect on what it is we are drawn to in others. Is it their soul, their fundamental self, or is it a set of traits that they appear to possess? I thought that was interesting. Do I still want to be with Jess because my relationship with them is on some sort of fundamental level rather than being based on their externality or a particular set of behaviours?

I feel like the podcast guest probably said this—it seems too poignant to be my own idea—but being so aware of someone else's frailties is forcing me to confront my own. It can be very overwhelming, but I am trying.

Later, on the way home from the office, I did some serious thinking. I often feel unreasonable and wrong in comparison to Jess, even when I'm sure my needs and wants are justified—and now that I am speaking more openly to other people, I am being reassured that they are, which is comforting. But when I voice my feelings and my anger to Jess, I feel small and completely unreasonable again. Another vicious cycle.

It is so strange how I can follow the same thought patterns over and over again but then suddenly find a fresh insight. Today I realised that Jess and I continue to cycle because I keep asking and expecting them to behave like a neurotypical person. I can't do that. They aren't like other people. Plus, they are in crisis, and that seems to be exacerbating their spectrum behaviours.

I also realised that I need to stop believing that Jess's version of everything is correct and mine is wrong. I need to have more trust and faith in myself.

When I got home I dressed carefully and put make-up on. I created a sunset eye by blending yellow, orange and pink across my lids and finished it off with blue mascara. I haven't worn eye make-up for months. It hasn't felt sensible given how much I've been crying.

I waited about an hour for Jess to arrive. I walked around the house to calm my nerves, but it didn't really help. I had thought about suggesting we walk to dinner, but as soon as Jess turned up, they were ready to go in the car, so I didn't mention it. I did ask if I could hug them, but they said they would prefer it if I didn't, so I didn't.

I tried to be nice and normal and to stick to my list of conversation topics. I told them the things that had been happening to me, silly things that I wanted them to know, like how the rat babies have disappeared. Jess started on their hormones six days ago but feels exactly the same so far. I told them I had been reading up on hormones again.

Dinner went okay on the whole, I thought. Jess bought me an ice cream after.

When we got back home I told them I had some other talking points. I could tell they were apprehensive. They sat on the blue chair opposite me, rather than their usual end of the couch. I tried to tell them about the realisation I'd had while driving home from work, but it felt hollow and stupid now.

Jess said they need all their energy for their own self-care. That they have tried to help me, to soften the blow, but they are sick of me saying that they are selfish and disappointing. That I was borderline gaslighting them. I feel as though they have been actual gaslighting me for a long time, but I didn't say anything, I just took it. I probably have been gaslighting them too.

I said I was sorry, that this whole thing was making me a horrible person and that all I have ever wanted was for them to be happy and confident and feel good. They said they knew this, but that I loved them too much to be good for either of us.

Jess doesn't think that we can recover if we keep seeing each other. They said that it would probably be some time before they would be ready to meet again. They came over to where I sat and held my hand before going to the door. I had tears streaming down my face, because this was it, the last time I would see them. I got up and followed them to the front door.

They turned and hugged me. They told me they loved me and that they were sorry. Our bodies still fit together so perfectly. I said I was sorry too and that I loved them so much.

We stood that way for a long time, holding each other and crying. Jess apologised once more, this time for not being strong enough, and promised to reach out when they were less angry. I told them they could call me any time and that I would be there for them. We said we loved each other once more and they left. They didn't look back.

I cried downstairs for a long time and then went upstairs to undress. I put on my dressing-gown then checked out the window to see if Jess was still out there. They were. I watched until the car pulled away. They must have been too emotional to drive straight away, which was comforting. Or maybe that wasn't it at all. I'm not sure.

I cried for a good while upstairs and then went down to the kitchen to make a cup of tea. When I'd calmed down I made myself finish my journal entry for the day. I am going to be more diligent about writing in my journal; I think it will help me.

Then I went to bed and cried there. I was half expecting Jess to text me goodnight, but they didn't.

10 January

Intentions
1. To get through the day
2. To go in to the office

Happenings
I've been feeling angry today.

I've been thinking again about what Jess said in their last email and in our last in-person conversation, about me gaslighting them, about me implying that they would be a better person if they could just love me or be with me. It's not that at all. It's actually that I refuse to believe that they are the type of person who would treat someone else so horribly. That they aren't behaving like the type of person I can respect. And that they have gaslit me throughout this whole process, made me feel as though my feelings and my loss is nothing in comparison

159

to their transition, that I am crazy for wanting to be seen and treated as an equal.

It doesn't matter how important any of this is to me; it will never stand up in comparison to who Jess is trying to become. I will always be second. If I am not a part of Jess's life, I will surely be shed along with the masculine part of their identity and I won't be there to find my place within their feminine one.

But I can't say any of this now because we are ceasing contact.

Also, I should probably just stop saying things because it never helps. It only makes everything worse.

Another thing I can't stop thinking about is being compared to Harrison and Lucas. My new theory is that it's a distancing and coping mechanism on Jess's part. I really don't think I am being unreasonable or denigrating those other relationships by finding the comparison hurtful. I have always wanted Jess to forge stronger connections with others and to strengthen their existing friendships. I've felt the burden of being the only person close to them.

Also, towards the end of our relationship, Jess would refer to our house as 'your house', which must have been another distancing mechanism. That used to really upset me but today it is pissing me off. It has always been *our* house.

Anyway, I know I need to stop fixating. All of these thoughts are very ugly.

I've found myself having an imaginary conversation with Jess in my head.

Jess: This is who I really am. Can you still love me?

Me: Yes, I can and I do.

Jess: Thank you.

Me: This is who I am. Can you still love me?

Jess: No, I don't have the capacity. I can only offer friendship.

Me: I understand, but that's not enough.

Jess: I resent that what I am offering isn't enough.

Me: Supporting each other, living together, sleeping together, being in a partnership is not equivalent to seeing each other for a few hours once a week, having zero physical contact and texting occasionally.

Maybe I could have actually moved towards a friendship if I had felt less.

After I calmed down I went into the office and got quite a lot done. We are about to start work on a new project that I will be in charge of, which will be a good distraction. In the afternoon I got a chilli hot chocolate to help me feel better. It worked ever so slightly.

I caught the tram home and just thought about things because I was too tired to read. I realised that I have been pinning a lot of hope on the hormones and Jess's physical transition. I hoped that once they feel more comfortable within their body they might be able to access their emotions in a different way and be able to connect with me again. But after doing more reading and after speaking with them last night, I have realised that even if such a thing were to happen, it would likely be years away. I don't know if I can wait that long.

I couldn't bring myself to make anything for dinner, so I ate a bag of microwave popcorn.

The bloody rat babies have turned up again. I hid the birdseed from them and alternately yelled at them and sprayed them with the hose, but they just don't seem to learn their lesson, the little bastards.

Grateful for

1. Chilli hot chocolate
2. Doing good work
3. Writing in my journal

11 January

Happenings

It's 4 a.m.-ish but I'm trying not to look at the time. I woke up because of the heat and a loud noise. Initially I thought I had knocked something off my bedside table, then I convinced myself there was a burglar, but after I mustered the courage to get up and check I discovered that a fat stack of magazines had fallen off the bookshelf. I put on the air conditioning and got back into bed, safe in the knowledge that no one was trying to bop me, and now I'm just lying here thinking and taking the proactive step of writing things down.

It is finally sinking in that I can't rely on Jess to help me through this time. I have to help myself. Jess wrote to me once that they can't be my solution. And in my depression-fuelled fog, I don't think I fully appreciated what that meant at the time.

Because they didn't communicate honestly, they have always known more and had more time to process. I've always been on the back foot when it comes to Jess, even before they first told me about being trans. I have felt so much guilt and shame for still needing to bridge that gap, for still needing to understand what had happened, for still needing to reach out to them. For grieving. Because we have been operating on different timeframes, we have been trying to pick up the pieces in isolation. Actually, we have each been scrambling to pick up very different pieces of what we had.

I have constantly compared myself to them and found myself wanting. But I could never have caught up. Nor should I have wanted to. I need to grieve. I can't rush that.

I had believed we were in a partnership, that we were equals. But we weren't equals really, not at the end. It's difficult not to feel taken advantage of when you have been so open and honest and the other person, despite their best intentions, has been deceitful. It's no wonder I have been questioning how much of our relationship was real. How much of it was me interacting with the persona Jess had carefully constructed and how much of it was their fundamental self?

Jess said that I put too much energy into thinking about what was real and what was fake, and that of course it had all been real. I am not so sure that is true. I think they might be trying to reassure themselves or to relieve their guilt. Or does that way of thinking negate all their experiences in a male body? That seems unfair.

I can see now that Jess reached their own conclusions about ceasing contact as a means to protect their mental health a long time before I did. And I think that conclusion centres around relieving the guilt they feel. I am still not sure that I have actually reached those conclusions for myself yet. But it has been forced upon me and I will have to do my best to reconcile with it.

I have a lot of problems that stem from no longer being needed. After being so important and vital to someone I now find myself unwanted and superfluous. The last night we saw each other, Jess urged me to work through what happened so that I could understand myself better, rather than working through it in order to explain myself to them or have them understand me.

And that is incredibly sensible. But I do still want Jess to understand me. Why do I need that? I still want them to know and love me for who I am. I guess it's part of being at a different stage of the grieving process from them. I think I have to accept that the person I knew and loved, the person who loved me, may not exist anymore, and that if I have the opportunity I may have to get to know a whole new person.

I also worry that I am softening or distancing myself from the damage of the last year. That slow, inexorable erosion of my self and my physicality. Not being touched, my needs being secondary. This has taken its toll and I need to look at it. The person I love is the same person who shut themselves off from me, who let me feel small, who took advantage of me, and I can't keep making excuses for that or pushing it aside. I need to examine it all up close and acknowledge the role I played.

Oh god, I just realised that I wanted Jess to save me! I can't believe it.

Anyway, this is more than enough thinking. I am thoroughly awake now. It's quite odd to be able to get up at a strange time in the morning and put the air conditioning on without having to consider anyone else's needs.

I never wanted to live alone.

Later

Susanne and I went to meet Casper the cat. He belongs to a friend of hers who is going on holidays and he is going to come and stay with me for a little while. Today we are checking that we get on and if that goes well he will be dropped off for an extended visit in a couple of days.

On the way I told Susanne about what happened between Jess and me on our last night, because of course Jess hadn't told her. She thought I was coping well so far, but I explained that was because we'd been working towards no contact, so it was not a complete shock—though it's still so recent that I am feeling numb. I surmised it would hit me at the one-week mark. After that, it would be the longest period of time we will have gone without speaking since we first got together over six years ago.

I explained that I am trying to think of this time apart as a way to express my love. If I love Jess as I say I do, then giving them this space is the greatest gift I can give. Susanne said that was admirable and something that not everyone can do. She also warned me that I need to be gentle on myself when I can't be loving in that way, because I won't be able to do it all of the time.

I talked to Susanne about being upset and worried about Jess's upcoming birthday. I still wanted to acknowledge it but wasn't sure how. I had thought about making Jess a card so that they have the option not to open it if they don't want to. I really wanted to make them something but Susanne said that was too romantic. She said it is important not to make Jess feel more guilty.

Maybe I'll draft a card message and then see how I feel.

The rest of the afternoon and evening I just lay around trying to read, and failing.

Our separation has shown me sides of myself that I don't like. I have given in to ugly, hateful outbursts that I have found confronting and repulsive. My pain has caused me to act in ways contrary to my nature. I have said and done things that I regret. It is such a complicated feeling to love someone in such an overwhelming way, to want to be with them so much it physically hurts, but to know that your presence causes them pain. At the same time, staying away, giving them the space they crave, causes you excruciating pain. It's an impossible balance between inflicting pain or suffering it, and who you end up choosing to hurt the most says a lot.

I think if I can uncover those things, the secrets I keep within myself, and confront them—especially those I am most ashamed of and don't want to admit to—then I will be able to heal. I think

Jess tried to bury so much for so long that it corroded them. I don't want that to happen to me.

I'm not well. My brain isn't functioning normally, it is trying to process so much while still going about the business of making me breathe and digest and attempt to get up and go to work and all that. So I can't expect too much of myself too soon.

In one of our sessions, Rachel said that it can be more straight-forward to process some forms of grief, such as that resulting from the death of a loved one or the end of a marriage, but something like the situation I find myself in is more complex and there isn't really a roadmap for untangling this particular relationship or coping with the resulting grief. Which explains why I sometimes wish Jess was dead. That's something I have never admitted properly before. Whenever I've had the thought I've quickly quashed it because it is too sickening and awful to feel as though everything would be easier to deal with if Jess had simply died.

It has been a big day and I've just realised that I forgot to do my intentions. They would have been:

1. Get through the day
2. Meet Casper the cat

I think my new journal is working out quite well. Imagine if I had got serious about journalling earlier! The epiphanies I could have had.

Grateful for

1. Having so many big revelations
2. Susanne and Casper the cat

12 January

Intentions

1. To get through the day

Happenings

After having been so active during the early morning the day before, I tried to sleep in today and woke up naturally at 8.30 a.m. I had one bad-ish dream where I was meant to be doing something with a bunch of people but after going back inside to get my water bottle I came out to find that they had driven off without me. I ran after their car but couldn't catch them.

I spent the morning reading with far more success than yesterday. I ate a chocolate bagel with a chocolate schmear and banana, which was quite lush. Nora came over for tea after she went to the dentist; she is looking after me because she is the best. We had lovely chats. But as grateful as I am to have my closest friends checking up on me, I find I just want Jess. Well, Jess in addition to them. And that makes me feel guilty sometimes.

In the afternoon I went over to see Mumma, Nanny and Poppy and all the cats. We were sad about Lizzie, who had made her nose bleed—there was blood all over her forearms and paws. I mowed Nanny and Poppy's lawn and thought of Jess while I did it. They used to love lawnmowers when they were little. I thought of how much I love Jess and what that love means to me. How I used to feel going about my business knowing they were at home or coming home to me. I thought of them and their body.

When I got home I lay on the couch for hours and just rested. I haven't really thought about my sexuality as much since Jess left. At first I was consumed by what being attracted to them in all their femme glory meant, but now I find it doesn't really matter to me in terms of my own identity.

Maybe I am queer, but I don't think I have the energy to investigate it properly right now. I can't imagine a future with other people or other bodies—all I can think about is Jess. So maybe I am pansexual or maybe I am just regular old heterosexual and this is purely about Jess.

I think the biggest impact this whole thing has had on my sexuality has been the complete erasure of it. As Jess became less comfortable with physical touch of any kind, I felt myself becoming increasingly uncomfortable in my own body. Rationally I knew it wasn't about me, and Jess would reassure me that it wasn't, but that didn't change how I felt.

For the most part, I was always more sexual than Jess. We had amazing sex. The best ever. But then we were faced with my appetite being the same while Jess's became practically non-existent, and the more I was rejected by them the more it felt as though there was something wrong with me—that my body was undesirable and that was the reason Jess didn't want me.

Eventually they stopped touching me at all, even innocuously. They stopped kissing me. If we did have sex it was because I had asked, had 'booked it' in advance, and even then it wasn't intimate. I usually felt worse afterwards, so I stopped asking. I became very ashamed of my sexual urges and I still carry that shame. I can't even masturbate anymore. If I try to, I cry and have to stop.

I suppose that's why I can't think about my sexuality or imagine what it might be. But I guess it's not all lost, because I do still think sexy things about Jess, and I do still want them. It's just that those feelings are now laced with mortification.

Maybe one day when I'm better I'll find more people who are queer and I'll talk to them and figure out who I am. I remember reading somewhere once that when your partner transitions, so do you. So maybe when I have more energy this will be the start of my own transition. I was talking to James the other day and he said that if I can imagine Jess and I living a life together as two women and that is something I truly want, then that is a queer desire.

I can imagine that. And I do want that. So maybe this is the start of something queer for me, which would mean that I am actually grieving the loss of two separate things:

1. The future I thought Jess and I were building together before they told me they were trans.
2. The new, queer future I made space for after that revelation.

Or maybe I'll realise I am exactly the same person I always was and this was just something unique to Jess and my love for them.

Anyway, I must talk to Rachel about all this in a session one day.

Oh my god, the other thing that happened today was that I actually found an online group for partners of trans people! I cannot believe that I finally found one! I requested to join and I was approved after talking to the moderator, but reading about all the other members who were still with their trans partners upset me too much. As happy as I am to have found the group, I don't think I am ready for it quite yet, although one day I hope I will be.

Grateful for
1. Nora
2. Home visit
3. Bagels
4. Trans partners group

13 January

Intentions
1. To get through the day
2. Welcome Casper

Happenings
I tried to get up earlier today but couldn't pull it off. It's getting harder and harder to get out of bed in the mornings. Sometimes it can take me up to an hour. If I didn't have to call Mumma and Nanny at eight o'clock every weekday morning to check in I don't know if I would get up at all.

I think it's a combination of fear and shame that drives me to make that call each morning. Shame for being so depressed that I can't get up. Fear that if Mumma actually knew how bad I was she would be upset and worried. Shame that I was the cause of the upset and worry.

I put all my energy into making that call, which gets me up and into the day, which is positive in a way. Plus, I like checking in with them. Nanny and Poppy were going grocery shopping. Mumma was going to work. The cats were all having a leisure day.

Once I got up I packed away my fake Jess in preparation for Casper the cat's arrival. I tried not to think about it as I took the blanket out of the bed and shoved it unceremoniously in the cupboard. When we had dinner that last night, Jess told me that I had to get rid of it, but I said I wasn't ready. Fake Jess has helped me so much at night, I'm not sure how I will sleep without them. At least Casper will be there instead.

I am missing them a lot today—the real Jess, that is. It's less acute, though, more a dull ache, a background to everything I do.

Casper arrived after work and he has settled in well so far. He has come with a lot of personal belongings, which is an adjustment. He is a beautiful cat, though, and he has bright blue eyes. Just like Jess.

I was thinking about something else that was said in that podcast episode I listened to the other day. The guest speaker talked about not quite believing that other people are interested in his confessions and the impact that has had on the way he views the permeability of boundaries, both of others and his own.

I have always been the recipient of other people's stories and secrets rather than the one doing the confiding. Perhaps it comes from being an introvert and therefore a natural observer. My listening skills are highly developed and I am generally good at offering advice. But now that I have big personal things to say, for the first time in a long time I am finding it hard to shift the dynamic in my relationships the other way and to become the person who talks rather than the one who listens.

I think I have viewed the boundaries of others as being more permeable than my own. It is more difficult to allow others to see my vulnerability, as I am not sure I have ever been perceived as someone who needs help. Maybe that is why it is so hard for me to ask my friends for help at the moment, or even identify when I need it.

Casper didn't come to bed with me. He is still adjusting. I made him three different beds to choose from. I can already tell we will get along nicely.

Grateful for
1. Having Casper
2. Being a bit more clear-headed

14 January

Intentions
1. To get through the day
2. To look after Casper

Happenings
According to my diary, today marks one year since the day Jess and I stayed up late to bleach their arm hairs. That was a very special

evening so I allowed myself to think about it. We sat together on the bathroom floor reading the instructions on the bottle of bleach I had bought and making up the bleach in batches. We talked about how Jess was feeling about their body, how uncomfortable they were within it, how they hoped that bleaching their coarse, dark arm hairs would help them to feel prettier. It took us a long time, and my back hurt so much, but what I loved most about that evening was being able to touch Jess, to be intimate with them. To be a part of things, to help them feel good within their body.

When we were done, Jess dressed femme and we lay together on the bedroom floor and I told them they were beautiful. I think that was a key time in my knowing I could do this and that I would find them attractive no matter what. That it was their essence I was drawn to.

I think it was also the first time I appreciated how powerful my ability to influence Jess's perception of themself was. I think I might have ultimately been wrong about the depth of that power, sadly. In the end it didn't matter how much I loved Jess, or how attractive I found them, it wasn't enough to change their opinion of themselves.

I went to Pilates at lunchtime in an effort to do some exercise. On the way back to the office I saw four old men having lunch together at the downstairs cafe. I have noticed them before. It was comforting to see them again. I like to imagine them having been friends forever, supporting each other through all life's big moments.

Hugh surprised me by being in. He was about to have a meeting with one our grant recipients. Danny, our casual, was also there, so while Hugh was at his meeting she and I went out for a late, long lunch at our favourite cafe, where we ordered our favourite dish: chickpea fritter, kale and a poached egg with dukkha, and a big pot of chai. I really like Danny and I wish we got to work together more often.

After Hugh and Danny went home I lay down on our office couch to rest. I had well and truly reached my work limit for the day. I can't seem to shake the feeling that Jess and I could be friends right now and still be seeing each other if it weren't for me. And that is an overwhelming amount of pressure. I am the one who is stopping us from having what we both want, which is to be in each other's lives. I honestly don't know how Jess can do it, how they can separate the relationship from the friendship. Perhaps I am asking too much of myself, but I do feel as though I am standing in the way of our mutual happiness. I do want to be Jess's friend. I want to be their best friend.

Susanne once told me when she came to visit that Jess doesn't miss the relationship. They miss me, they miss our home, but not the relationship. Hearing that was like a punch in the stomach. I still want Jess to *want* to be in a relationship with me. It hurts that they don't love me in that way, that they don't miss me in that way, that they don't miss what we had as a couple.

The cause of my deepest pain and shame is that the person I love stopped loving me. It might have been because of all that is going on inside Jess, or perhaps it was because I somehow ceased to be lovable. Maybe Jess never really loved me to begin with and they were just trying a relationship on. I don't know anymore.

Maybe I don't love Jess as they are. Maybe I actually want them to be someone else. I am asking them to be someone who can love me. And that isn't fair.

Eventually I packed up and went home. I find it so difficult to focus on anything other than what happened. All these thoughts and feelings just swim around my head constantly. There is no chance of escape and I am grateful for the occasional reprieve at work. It frustrates me but I have given up fighting this part of my depression. I have realised this is something I have to work with, not against, if I want to get through it.

Casper was waiting for me on the stairs when I got in, which was very sweet. He really is a beautiful cat, with his regal stripes and clear blue eyes. I mostly just lay on the couch and half watched TV this evening. Casper sat on the ottoman opposite me and I made kissy faces at him and told him I loved him. Maybe I will get my own kitty cat one day. An old one that needs a nice home to live out its days but doesn't make a mess or scratch the furniture.

I just realised I haven't cried today, which is a real first. My feelings about this are mixed.

On the one hand:

- It's good not to cry, obviously.
- I have been so dehydrated from all this crying.

- I have a weird rash around my eyes from so much crying.
- So much crying is really exhausting.
- Ceasing to cry is a sign my antidepressant dosage is probably right.

On the other hand, I don't really want to move on from Jess because I want to continue to love them just as much. Not that a lack of tears is any indication of moving on or loving them less. But still.

Grateful for
1. Casper
2. Hugh and Danny

15 January

Intentions
1. To get through the day
2. Reach out to friends
3. Prepare for work trip

Happenings
I tried to get up early again. I managed a whole ten minutes earlier than yesterday, so that's something. I am having a challenging morning. I am finding it difficult to focus and am feeling tired and sad. And it hasn't even been a whole week of no contact yet.

Today would have been our six-year-and-five-month anniversary. I used to love acknowledging our anniversary every month, until Jess got so annoyed by my anniversary enthusiasm that I had to restrict myself to half-yearly and then eventually just yearly. Maybe I did love Jess too much.

Actually, I am a loving person who likes to celebrate things, so I am not going to beat myself up for that.

I had a moment of weakness in front of the fridge this morning and cried over all of the abandoned condiments. Seeing the Sweet Baby Ray's barbecue sauce, the wholegrain mustard and the special blueberry and violet jam—those poor little jars full of condiments that I would never, could never, eat myself, now left to go mouldy—reminded me of my own abandonment.

After I recovered I went into the office and told Hugh, whom I was meeting for lunch, about the condiments. He laughed.

Hugh: Just throw them in the bin!
Me: I can't do that to them—it's not their fault they were abandoned.

Hugh couldn't understand how I could ascribe human feelings to inanimate objects.

After we had eaten, Hugh told me that our grant program is going to expand and that I will have to manage a team of people as well as more relationships with external researchers. It is quite exciting. I was worried about taking on more responsibility given my precarious emotional state, but Hugh said I had everyone's full support. I wanted so much to be able to tell Jess but of course I didn't. After Hugh left I went for a chilli hot chocolate and called Mumma to tell her. I was tempted to call Susanne, but then I thought that might just be using her as a surrogate for Jess, which wouldn't be fair to her, so I refrained.

I wrote on my to-do list for the day that I should reach out to my friends, so I sent them all a photo of Casper the cat and had some nice conversations. Xan is now going to come over on the weekend to spend the day with me.

The only other thing that happened today was that I had a spectacular revelation about something that happened a few years ago. For some reason, I was thinking about this super old, gross cardigan I sometimes like to wear. I used to keep it at Jess's old house to act as my surrogate dressing-gown when I slept over. Thinking about that cardigan got me thinking about the shelf I used to keep my clothes and underwear on, which got me thinking about the cupboard in general, which eventually led me to an incident that happened when I tried to lend Susanne the suitcase Jess kept at the bottom of that cupboard.

Jess was in the shower and I had gone downstairs to make some tea and got chatting to Susanne. She was about to go away for work but had no suitcase and I was like, 'Just borrow Jess's!' So I ran up and got it and brought it down to show her. She thought it was perfect, so I went back upstairs with my tea and thought nothing more of it.

When Jess came out of the shower I told them I had lent the suitcase to Susanne and they became incredibly angry. Jess asked if Susanne or I had looked in it and I said no, and they raced downstairs to retrieve it. Initially I was shocked because the reaction was so extreme, but then I thought that Jess must be hiding a present in it for me because our anniversary was coming up.

But today, as I recalled that baggy brown cardigan, I realised that of course it wasn't a present that they were hiding in that suitcase: it was girl things. The evening that I first saw Jess femme, they pulled that suitcase out from underneath our bed and unpacked all of their girl things to show me. I am certain now that it was probably lingerie, stockings and dresses that Jess was trying to hide from Susanne and me all those years ago.

This realisation actually made me quite angry, because I can also remember being upset when a present didn't materialise. I never brought the incident up, initially because I didn't want to spoil the surprise, and then later because I was embarrassed about my previous excitement. I'm sure Jess was relieved by my silence.

I also think that part of maintaining that silence was about preserving an idea I had of Jess: that they were the type of person who would buy their girlfriend a surprise gift. The longer I stayed quiet, the longer I could put off admitting they weren't really that person at all.

I packed my bags for my work trip tomorrow and went to bed. As I lay there, I thought about Jess's birthday, about everything that happened on their birthday last year. I still don't know what to do about acknowledging it this year. I've got my draft birthday letter ready just in case. I might ask Susanne again if there are any plans. I could give her all the abandoned condiments to pass on to Jess.

Also, the rat babies were out and about again. I sprayed them with the hose, the fuckers.

Grateful for
1. Casper
2. Hugh
3. Chilli hot choc
4. Seeing a rat baby carry a leaf
5. Spraying it with the hose

16 January

Intentions
1. To have a nice day
2. To visit my colleagues
3. To do good work

Happenings
I managed to wake up on time, thank god. I had five alarms set to make sure. And I made Mumma promise to call to make sure I was awake. Casper was still asleep on his cushion at the bottom of the bed. Seeing him curled up there was reassuring. I got ready in plenty of time, so I wrote Susanne a cute note about looking after Casper.

I was catching the bus up to Sydney so had asked Mumma to drop me at the station. It turned out that the driver had forgotten to turn up, so we were running very late. A homeless lady asked me not to stand so close to her while I was waiting so I decided to go pee at the office instead. At least the wait meant I could save myself from the horrible bus toilet. When the driver finally arrived and we were allowed to board I found myself having to sit next to someone. He was very sweaty and took lots of photos, both of himself and the scenery. Someone started snoring almost immediately. It was a bad trip on the whole.

I didn't have the energy to read so I ended up just thinking about Jess and making myself upset. I nearly cried a couple of times but got myself back together. I kept oscillating between being the magnanimous, loving person I want to be and giving in to the more ungenerous feelings of how unfair it all is, how poorly I've been treated and how much I don't want any of this.

When I arrived in Sydney, I walked to our new office. It is bigger and airier, so much better than our old one. I had a very productive day doing all sorts of productive things. Izra, Cameron and I had a breakthrough on one of our shared projects and were immodest telling the others how brilliant we were. Well, I was immodest and told the others how brilliant we were. It's nice to feel good about something. I hadn't felt that pleased with myself for a long, long time.

After work I had a solo fancy dinner, checked in to the hotel and then popped out for a special dessert. It was late-night shopping, so I went to our favourite bookshop. I still checked Jess's favourite sections out of habit. I saw one of the books I knew they wanted and got a bit emotional. I managed to buy myself a book from my reading list before leaving quickly.

It was a relief to be away from our home, the museum of our relationship. To be in a different city, just doing things for myself with no prospect of accidentally running into Jess. I've developed a fear of running into them ever since we broke off contact. On the tram, on the street. I've stopped meeting the gaze of other people when I am out, just in case. I mentioned it to Susanne and she couldn't understand why I would be afraid of seeing Jess because I love them and I've seen them a zillion times before. Apparently they are afraid of running into me too.

I wasn't quite sure how to explain it at the time, but I think I can now. The reason I am afraid is *because* I have seen them a zillion times. I know every line on their face, every mark on their body, as well as I know my own. I especially miss the little birthmark on their arm, the hollow between their clavicles, their funny curly toes and their perfect eyebrows. Their beautiful blue eyes.

And now I can't see any of it. I am scared that if I run into them, they will have changed—their hair will be longer, their face will have softened, breasts will be forming—and I will have missed all of it. I can't bear the thought that so many important things will have happened without me. There will be a physical representation of the time we have spent apart—time that I didn't want to spend apart.

As awful as that prospect is, it's not only that which bothers me. I am afraid of catching in their face a flicker of horror when they recognise me, of feeling the crushing realisation that they don't want to see me and they don't love me and that they wish they could be anywhere else. It's knowing that I would cry and cause a scene and somehow make everything worse, and because I'd be on the tram or wherever I couldn't escape.

I wish I could have seen Jess a few times a week like I asked. That way I wouldn't have any of these feelings. The longer this goes on, the less I can imagine that we will ever be able to meet again in a normal way. Too much has happened and none of it in a way that would have helped me. We are still doing exactly what Jess wants, the way they want it, right down to this no contact business. And look where it's got us. Two people who meant everything to one another now afraid of running into each other.

I checked in with Susanne before bed and she said Casper was totally fine.

Grateful for
1. Being away
2. Alone time
3. Everyone at work

17 January

Intentions
1. To do good work

Happenings
I went for breakfast at M&N's. Jess and I had breakfast here once on an anniversary trip. Being here doesn't hurt as much as

I thought it would. I used to have a physical reaction when I came to places like this or even thought of doing things that we had previously done together. But that is starting to dull. Maybe the increased dose on my meds is finally kicking in.

While waiting for my food, I decided that I am just going to own that I still love Jess. I carried a lot of shame about that before. Jess was always telling me I shouldn't love them because they were horrible, and everyone else was telling me that I had to let Jess go or at least take active steps towards letting them go because Jess clearly couldn't treat me properly. But I know Jess is a good person who has big troubles and isn't coping, and I'm going to let myself be where I'm at and not be ashamed of it. And where I am at is still in love, so I'll just let Jess go in my own time without forcing it.

I had a really lovely breakfast and chai while reading my book. I got some weird tomato thing on a pretentious pea puree which was actually quite delicious. I tried to eat and drink slowly and mindfully and to take pleasure in it. Being by myself and treating myself. Then I went to work and had another productive day.

When it was time to go home I had to rush for the bus and only just made it. I was so hot from all the fast walking that I had to take off my jacket and I discovered that I had ripped my shirt, which made me very sad. I had two seats to myself this time, so I spread out to read my book and eat an entire packet of chocolate-covered apricots for dinner.

While I was at work today Cameron and I had a very in-depth non-work-related discussion about sexuality, gender and dating, and on the bus I thought about femininity and feminine expression.

Over time, as Jess settled into their new identity, their gestures and expressions became ultra girly and, if I am very honest, it made me uncomfortable. I think it is because this kind of hyper-femininity doesn't match that of myself or the women I see around me. Jess's demeanour seemed like more of a romanticised version of a young woman, perhaps.

I've never given much thought to the way I express my femininity or my sexuality. I don't have to. That is my position of privilege. I think I'm aware of the effect I can have on people; I am aware of how I can use my identity as a woman and aspects of my physicality to get what I want from certain men. I think I am a very feminine person, but I've never been hyper girly or overtly sexual in my presentation or gestures. But I guess I've been lucky enough to just feel feminine naturally as I grew up, rather than having to build an identity from scratch by trying things out and pushing the boundaries of gender expression as Jess is now doing.

I think I secretly wished that Jess would be the same sort of person fundamentally, even as a girl. They were never super masculine in their physicality or expression anyway; I wouldn't have liked it if they were. They were just more neutral, really. But now they seem to be swinging hard towards the femme side of gender expression and I find that difficult to relate to.

This isn't something I would ever talk to Jess about—it would hurt them too much while they are figuring things out. It makes me a bit sick to question their femininity and how they choose to express it. Even though we aren't speaking to one another it still feels like a betrayal. Anyway, who am I to tell anyone how to be a woman or what it means to be one?

Casper was so happy to see me when I got home. And it's such a relief not having to come home to an empty house. I gave him his dinner and lots of pats.

Grateful for
1. Work
2. Chocolate-covered apricots
3. Being able to read
4. Casper being happy to see me

18 January

Intentions
1. To rest

Happenings
This morning I slept right up until Mumma came to get me. Casper was there on the bed. I blew him a kiss and patted the air near him because I couldn't actually reach him.

We went to the farmers' market. It was the first one for the year and lots of our favourite stalls were there. The fish people, the pasta man, the bagel people. It was nice to catch up with them all. Ever since Jess left I have kept buying all the same quantities at the market because I can't bring myself to tell any of the stall-holders that there is only me now, that I only need one piece of fish, not two. In addition to more food than I can actually eat, I did buy a few new plants for the garden. Mumma picked out a pretty pink one for me.

When I got home to unpack and get ready for work I discovered that Casper had knocked down one of my plants and the pot was broken. I saved the plant but the pot was completely smashed. I had to clean it all up so he didn't try to go to the toilet in the dirt while I was gone and was almost late for work as a result. I told Casper I was incredibly mad at him.

I thought about Jess at work. I indulged myself by imagining that they had finally decided that they wanted me but I had come to the conclusion that I no longer wanted them. That I would say all the things I had been rehearsing: 'You broke my heart, I begged you to stay, to love me, and you couldn't. You left me alone for too long and now I don't want you anymore.' And then they would beg me and I wouldn't cave in. I think this little fantasy is all about being in a position of power for once.

But of course I would still have them back in a heartbeat, which makes me a little disappointed in myself.

When I got home I spent the afternoon reading. I've now realised that the reason I was struggling to get through a teeny novella the other week is that my depression has killed my ability to read. Narratives I am unfamiliar with seem to require too much energy; there is too much uncertainty for me to handle on top of everything else. I have switched to rereading old favourites and that has been much better. In the book I am reading at the moment, I got to the part where the two main characters accidentally kiss. It wasn't a super sexy scene, but as I read it I felt that same swoopy feeling in my tummy that I often got as I kissed Jess. I thought about kissing them and I softened. I don't seem to be able to stay angry for long.

I'm getting a bit worried about money. I have been making do on my sole income. In a way, it's a financial blessing being too depressed to go anywhere or do anything. I am struggling to pay off the last of my credit card debt, though. I do have a McQueen blazer I'm not too emotionally connected to. And a pair of Chanel pumps I wouldn't cry about if I sold them. Maybe I will ask Timmy about selling them through her work. But nothing else. Hopefully I will get a pay rise when I officially start my expanded responsibilities at work! That would be amazing.

I still wish I could share my clothes with Jess. I have given them a few bits and bobs of mine over the years, both before and after their disclosure, but we never got to the point where we could share. It is going to cost Jess so much money to build a whole new wardrobe. New casual clothes, new going out clothes, new work clothes, new shoes. Bags, dresses, coats. If we were actually still in contact, and I didn't have financial problems, I would give them anything of mine they wanted. Well, the pieces that don't fit me or aren't part of my collection. My dream is to share. To have the dressing room as a play space for us both.

I made myself a proper dinner tonight—a piece of fish from the markets. It was a real ordeal, but I did it. I miss Jess's cooking so much. They always said that cooking for me was one of the ways they showed me love.

It's strange writing this journal. It makes me aware of how all over the place I am—not just day to day, but within a day. I wonder if that is normal. I might ask Rachel.

Grateful for

1. Managing to make dinner
2. Casper—when he doesn't break my bloody pots

19 January

Intentions

1. To have a better day than yesterday
2. To spend time with Xan

Happenings

Last night I dreamed that Jess and I were trying to have sex. It was our second attempt—in the dream, that is—our first attempt not having gone so well. Jess was able to climax faster the second time, but I wasn't able to at all.

> *Dream Jess:* Well, I think that went better.
> *Me:* Yes, I think so [even though it hadn't really been good for me].
> *Dream Jess:* You don't think I am doing this for you, do you?

I can't remember the exact words Dream Jess said now but that was the gist of it: they were just using me to get back into the swing of things sexually. I think if Casper hadn't walked all over me and woken me up at that precise moment I would have been much more upset about it.

I got up and had a bagel for breakfast and bobbled about for a bit. Xan arrived while I was watering the garden. I made tea and we drank it outside. Then we came inside and coloured in. We talked about lots of different things. Work, depression, houses, money, therapy. It was lovely to colour while talking about difficult things. Soothing. Casper sat with us. He responded very well to Xan.

We walked slowly up to town for lunch. We both had spiced eggs and toast. Then we walked slowly back to finish our colouring. As we walked I talked about some of the things I had been feeling about Jess. I felt better, in the same way I often do when I speak to Susanne—like I am a normal person.

I said to Xan, All I can do for Jess is say, *I love you, I am here for you*, and just hope that they will reach out to me again one day. I don't know how long to keep hoping and waiting, or if I even should be. But I do know that, right now, I don't want to be with anyone else. Maybe that will change one day, but I'm not going to force it. I have to focus on looking after myself in the meantime.

After Xan went home I had a shower. I did a body scrub, a double cleanse, a scalp treatment. I did it all. I am officially clean. Then I cooked my second piece of fish for dinner. It turned out quite well.

The rat babies came back, and I yelled at them.

Tonight I came across something that Jess had written to me. After it had become clear that they had withheld so much of themselves for so long, we had tried to do an exercise from a relationship book Susanne had recommended to help us reconnect with one another. We had to answer a set of questions, give them to each other and then discuss them. Very little of what I had to say came as a surprise to Jess, however much of what I learned from their answers was shocking and saddening. Admissions about Jess's self-loathing, their fear, the depth of their despair and disconnect.

I've been thinking about one part in particular. Jess wrote:

> Where I should have been open and honest about myself I chose instead to keep up my wall, to pretend that I'm more together than I am, to hope that this, when combined with the healing properties of a proper relationship, would fix me. The more I committed to this role the harder it has become to undo it. Worse still, I fear there is a genuine possibility that my partnership will not allow me to become the person I want to be (assuming I am even capable of doing so), or that it cannot survive my becoming. Know that I am sorry for the way I have treated you up to this point, and that I will continue to feel sorry forever after. Know that I love you and that the concern I feel for you during this is almost paralysing, and that I hate myself for not being able to express it through warmth or understanding.

It is heartening in a way that Jess was afraid that our partnership would not survive their becoming because it meant that they valued it enough to be afraid of losing it. But it is absolutely heartbreaking to read those words again now knowing, from my perspective at least, that the relationship could have survived it.

Although at times it has felt like it, deep in my heart I don't think Jess has ever acted maliciously towards me. Reading all of those answers back now, I know Jess is a broken person who is deeply unhappy and that this is something they will have to work through for themself. I could never have saved them.

Jess once told me that without my love and without my support they would never have had the strength to confront their true identity. Even if that ultimately meant that they then had the strength to leave me, to explore that on their own, in their own way, I think I can be proud that I could give them that gift.

After reading Jess's words I cried for a long time because I still love Jess just the same and I miss them so much.

I don't think I will send the birthday letter.

Grateful for
1. Xan
2. Casper
3. The garden looking really nice

20 January

Intentions
1. To get back on track at work
2. To start preparing myself for Jess's birthday
3. To make my confession

Happenings

I was thinking a lot about Jess before I got up this morning. I was in that funny state when you are both asleep and awake and your thinking is part conscious, part unconscious. I seemed to be mixing thoughts about work with thoughts about my personal situation and it was almost amusing how seriously my sleepy brain was taking the exercise.

Something we discussed during my last work trip was the assumptions we have made about what we do, the environment we operate within and our ability to affect change within our work universe. I have to give feedback on a strategy document today but instead of thinking about that my brain was running through some of my personal assumptions and why I had made them.

My assumption: Our entire relationship was false.
The basis: Jess was lying to themselves and to me.

My assumption: Our entire relationship was genuine.
The basis: It didn't feel false at the time.

My assumption: Jess doesn't love me anymore.
The basis: They said so and they left.

My assumption: Jess does still love me.
The basis: Jess said that the depth of their feelings had not changed, they just couldn't express them in the same way right now.

My assumption: Jess does not miss me.

The basis: They left, they continue to stay away and maintain the no contact rule.

My assumption: Jess does miss me.

The basis: Susanne told me.

And on and on it went, contradictory assumptions about my company, my body, my behaviour until I was properly awake and thoroughly sick of myself.

Can all these assumptions coexist? Do any of them have any basis in truth? I can't actually test any of them because we are no longer in contact with each other. Would it even be a good idea to test any of them? Is Jess in a position to know what they want?

After feeding and patting Casper I went into the office and managed to get through most of the tasks on my to-do list. I played music and podcasts on the speaker while I worked and made lots of tea.

When I got home I just lay on the couch and read. Casper was being very sweet and meowsing around. I didn't even look to see what the rat babies were doing so they got the night off. I was too distracted by my guilt about the horrible thing that happened between Casper and me last night, which I have been repressing. But I am not doing repression anymore so I am going to get it off my chest.

Casper was sitting on the ottoman and I was sitting on the couch. We were looking at each other and as I looked into his blue eyes I felt a burst of anger flare so brightly in my chest that I had the strongest urge to hurt him. I wanted to squeeze him tight until he burst.

I hadn't moved and he hadn't moved, but I had pictured causing him pain so vividly I was afraid. I couldn't look at him or touch him for the rest of the evening. I didn't think I would actually hurt him, but the hatred and anger I had felt for him in that moment scared me.

I have been thinking about it all day because it is so upsetting. I have just been googling 'what does it mean if I want to hurt my pet' and found articles about cute aggression, serial killers and people having suffered trauma.

I got stuck down a slightly gross Freudian rabbit hole but thankfully realised that it wasn't Casper I wanted to hurt, it was Jess, and those beautiful blue eyes that they share were my trigger. So that is a relief. I would just die if I turned out to be the type of person who hurts the poor innocent cat they are meant to be taking care of. I will see what Rachel thinks next time I see her.

After all that I went up to bed and spent a long time looking at the photo of Jess and me on my bedside table. I haven't been able to bring myself to put it away. I am not even sure if I want to put it away, although I probably should. The photo was taken at our old boss's retirement party. I can still remember that night so distinctly: it was the night I knew I really liked Jess and that I wanted something to happen between us. We had been physically close that whole evening at the party and when a group of us went to the after-party drinks Jess and I sat next to each other. When Mumma came to pick me up at some point early in the morning, I kissed Jess goodbye on the cheek.

Jess always hated how they looked in that photo, which of course makes sense now. I thought they looked incredible, but they have always made me melt no matter how they look. When I look at that photo, I don't think about our appearance—I simply remember how I felt about this beautiful and mysterious person who I wanted to get to know and who seemed to want to get to know me. As my hand grazed their shoulders and my lips brushed their cheek, I felt that thrill of possibility in my stomach. I knew something would happen. I knew I would spend time with this person.

That's what this photo shows me: two people on the precipice of love and happiness. And I want those feelings back.

Grateful for
1. Not actually hurting Casper
2. Not wanting to hurt him anymore

21 January

Intentions
1. To have a shower
2. To get through the day
3. To prepare myself for tomorrow

Happenings

It's Jess's birthday eve.

I didn't sleep very well. I know I had a bad dream, but I can't remember what it was now. I just know I had to wake myself up from it.

After I fed Casper I went straight back to bed. I read for a little while and then made myself have a shower. I knew if I didn't do it this morning I wouldn't do it at all. Casper watched from the bathmat. It was just as well I managed to get into the shower because standing under the water I had a very important epiphany.

I've noticed that I've been framing everything that has unfolded as my own failing. I can't separate romantic love from friendship. I can't create a home environment that Jess feels they can stay in. I can't help Jess become who they want to be.

While I was in the shower getting all upset, I decided to try to look at it another way. Jess is currently unable to be intimate. Jess is currently unable to connect physically. Jess can't support me right now, even as a friend. Jess can't communicate clearly with me.

And given all that they are going through with their transition, of course they can't do those things. It is unfair of me to expect that of them.

So then I spiral back around to feeling unreasonable and framing everything as my fault for expecting too much or wanting the wrong thing.

But, again, what if I reframe that? I am only human. I may be an empath, but that doesn't mean I have a superpower. Jess has been asking me to do an impossible thing. I am *still* asking myself to do that impossible thing—the thing I tried to do for over a year and couldn't manage: to be a friend and not a partner.

Because I have carried so much guilt and shame regarding this particular perceived failure of mine, I then had a go at framing what I was able to do in a positive way.

- I was able to understand and articulate my own needs.
- I was able to communicate my needs clearly.
- I was able to love unconditionally.
- I was able to discover and embrace a new aspect of my sexuality.
- I was able to support the person I love in a time of crisis.
- I was able to help them connect with themself in a way they hadn't before.
- I was able to give them moments where they felt comfortable and confident within their body.

When I look at that list, I can see that I was able to do a lot of good. And I feel proud of that. Even now, as I write this, my inner voice says, *It wasn't enough, you aren't able to be friends, you aren't able to be there for them now*, but I have to keep fighting that.

And here is the epiphany part: the qualities that allowed me to do those things are the same qualities that prevent me from being friends now. And if I had to be one or the other, I would choose being able to give what I did because that was bigger and more meaningful than being friends now. Although, of course, I do wish we could have had both.

I still think that if we could figure ourselves out we could be happy together. If we could have a relationship where we were truly equals, where Jess was honest with me, where we came together as our authentic selves, it could be magical. Before all this we were so well suited. We helped each other to be better people, we cared so much about each other, got along so well, were so sexually compatible. It was Jess confronting their true self and how we respectively handled that confrontation that broke us.

I think this is why I can barely bring myself to have a shower these days: it can be an exhausting place for big thinking. That and I rarely have the energy to take off my clothes to get in there.

I went back to bed to write all this. Then I dragged myself into the office and did my best at work. Which, given the day, wasn't very good. But it was something.

Susanne came over to see me when I got home, which was very kind. She knew what a hard day it was going to be for me tomorrow. I told her about the big thinking I did this morning and explained that I've decided not to send the birthday letter. I am going to respect Jess's desire that we have no contact.

She said something to me that I thought was quite beautiful. If we were to equate my mental illness to a physical one, I have been in the intensive care unit of a hospital. Things have been touch and go, and I have needed round-the-clock attention and support. Now that I am showing some signs of improvement, I can be moved to a ward. While I am still in the hospital and I still need a lot of care, it's no longer critical.

And maybe in a few months' time I will leave the ward. I won't be the same as I was before, but I will be out and about. I'll still have regular check-ups, but these will become less and less frequent until, one day, probably years from now, I won't need them at all.

I thought about that in bed, and I thought about Jess and how I really do hope they have a nice day tomorrow.

Getting better is not linear, and while my overall trajectory might be incrementally upwards, it is filled with many stumbles and scrambles that I must claw my way back from. While I am feeling all philosophical and loving today, tomorrow will be awful and I am going to slip backwards. Probably a long way backwards.

But the difference is, this time I am prepared. This time I am ready to get back up again.

Grateful for
1. Susanne
2. Actually having a shower
3. Being ready

POSSIBILITY

22 January

Letter, unsent:

Dear Jess,

Happy Birthday. I hope you are having a peaceful day.

Thank you for sharing yourself with me. Thank you for trusting me. Thank you for spending time with me. I am grateful for everything we had and I don't regret any of it.

I know I said I would always be there for you, but to do that right now would be doing myself an injustice. I don't know how long this will be the case, but at least for now, we cannot be friends. After everything we have had, and given everything I still want and hope for, a friendship isn't enough, and is too painful for me.

I have always and will always want you to be happy and to feel whole. You are kind, brave, smart, funny, playful and alluring.

You deserve to have everything you want and I do hope you can find it.

I also hope that we can find each other again one day.

Love always,
Emma

ACKNOWLEDGEMENTS

It takes a village, as they say, and *Now That I See You* is no exception.

To my family (and cats), thank you for loving me, supporting me and making sure I eventually got out of bed each day.

To my colleagues at work, thank you for being flexible with me during my extended period of personal crisis. Being able to work when I could enabled me to keep going both physically and emotionally and literally kept me in my house.

Susanne, thank you for putting yourself in an incredibly uncomfortable position through each and every draft and for championing me and this story. I could not have done this without you.

Esther, whose writing and mind I have always admired, your feedback was instrumental to this work.

Lauren, I owe you so much. I will always be grateful for everything I have learned about myself as a person with your help.

To Amber, Carol, Cleo, Ellen, Holly, Kara, Karim, Lexi, Merrillee, Ruby and Vicki, who read early drafts and gave me feedback, your support and assurance has made this story what it is.

To Becca, James, Jenna, Gen, Howard and Miriam, thank you for going above and beyond.

To everyone at Allen & Unwin, especially Annette, Christa, Tessa, Jenn, Maggie and Sandra, thank you for guiding me through this process and helping me to develop as a writer and author. Ali, your feedback and kindness has meant so much to me. Thank you to Sandy for my beautiful cover and to my typesetter for laying everything out so beautifully.

As someone who has come from a scientific background and has long struggled with prioritising their creative skills and urges, thank you to *The Australian*, Vogel's and Allen & Unwin for valuing my work as a writer. I am deeply honoured to be part of this community and to be recognised in this way.

And finally to Jesse. Thank you for everything, especially for your support in sharing parts of our story. You are my muse and I love you mega.